Tonight, she was tempted to sleep naked and fantasize about him.

"I better go now."

"All right, but when are we going to see each other again?"

In her dreams, Mary thought. Or maybe it would be in her nightmares. She was getting hooked on a man who'd helped hurt her mother. Even if he hadn't done it purposely.

"When, Mary?" Brandon asked again.

"I don't know." Her confusion was growing by leaps and bounds. "Let's figure it out later."

"Okay." He leaned in to kiss her again. But this time, it was gentlemanly, a protective peck on the cheek. "Will you text me to let me know you got home safe?"

She nodded, then turned to open her car door. She climbed behind the wheel and locked herself inside, afraid that she would never be safe again.

* * *

Nashville Secrets is part of the
Sons of Country series from
Sheri WhiteFeather!

Dear Reader,

Are you a good secret keeper? I don't know if I am. My oldest sister is the best. If you tell her something and ask her not to repeat it, she will keep silent for sure. I've always admired her for that. This story has lots of secrets. But the title is *Nashville Secrets*. It's also the third and final book in my Sons of Country series. I've gotten so close to this fictional family, I feel as if they are my own. Maybe I can revisit them in the future. A spin-off, perhaps? Only time will tell.

Love and hugs,

Sheri WhiteFeather

SHERI WHITEFEATHER

NASHVILLE SECRETS

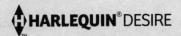

Recycling programs
for this product may
not exist in your area.

ISBN-13: 978-1-335-60352-4

Nashville Secrets

Printed in U.S.A.

www.Harlequin.com

Sheri WhiteFeather is an award-winning, bestselling author. She lives in Southern California and enjoys shopping in vintage stores and visiting art galleries and museums. She is known for incorporating Native American elements into her books and has two grown children who are tribally enrolled members of the Muscogee Creek Nation. Visit her website at www.sheriwhitefeather.com.

Books by Sheri WhiteFeather

Harlequin Desire

Billionaire Brothers Club

Waking Up with the Boss
Single Mom, Billionaire Boss
Paper Wedding, Best Friend Bride

Sons of Country

Wrangling the Rich Rancher
Nashville Rebel
Nashville Secrets

Visit her Author Profile page at Harlequin.com, or sheriwhitefeather.com, for more titles.

One

Mary McKenzie sat on a bench in the downtown Nashville park, with a view of the river, waiting for Brandon Talbot to appear. He walked his dog here every Sunday, just after daybreak. She hadn't met him yet, but she knew all sorts of things about him.

Brandon was a classically handsome, highly successful attorney, oozing with sophistication. He was also the man she was supposed to seduce. Not to the point of sleeping with him. Heaven help her, she would never do that. But it would be a seduction just the same.

Maybe she would get lucky and Brandon wouldn't show up. Or maybe he would have one of his glamorous lovers with him. That would certainly get her off the hook.

She glanced up and saw him in the distance, just him and his canine companion, a Siberian husky with a silvery coat. Should she abort this insane mission and go home?

No, she thought. If she quit now, she would be excusing the pain his lying, cheating, country superstar dad had caused her mom, as well as what Brandon himself had done.

Mary returned to the book she was pretending to read. Typically, she liked to read. It was one of her favorite pastimes. But for the past few Sundays, she'd been using it as her cover while she spied on him. A lone girl with her nose buried in a book, a persona that actually fit her quite well.

She waited, trying to time her approach so it seemed natural. Finally, she closed the book and put it in her bag. She stood, as if she was preparing to leave the park.

As she headed in Brandon's direction, she wished that she didn't find him so attractive. The last thing she needed was a crush on the enemy.

She adjusted her cardigan over her blouse. The early-morning air was a bit chilly. The month of June could be funny that way.

She kept going, getting nearer to Brandon. He was wearing a gray pullover, sweatpants and pricey sneakers. By now, she could see the logo on his shoes.

Once they were close enough to make polite eye contact, she lifted her gaze, and he nodded a silent greeting. If Mary didn't know better, she would mistake him for a good guy. His demeanor was friendly. She tried to seem friendly, too.

Seizing the opportunity to speak to him, she said, "I've seen you here before, and I've been meaning to tell you how beautiful your dog is." She'd been practicing that line for weeks, readying herself for this moment.

Brandon smiled, so composed, so freaking gorgeous. He stood tall, with lean muscles, jet-black hair and piercing blue eyes. Mary's heart was pounding so hard, she feared it would pop out of her chest and roll straight into the river.

"Thanks," he replied. "His name is Cline."

She already knew the dog's name. She'd seen tons of pictures of him on Brandon's Instagram. "I'd love to have a husky. But I share an apartment with my sister. It's a cute little place, but there's barely room for the two of us, let alone a big dog." Mary decided her best course of action was to mix lies with the truth, and their cozy apartment was the truth. "Is it okay if I pet him?"

Brandon nodded. "Sure."

She knelt to stroke the husky's thick fur. He stood patiently, highly trained and wonderfully behaved. "Look at those eyes. They're so blue." Like his master's, she thought. But she wasn't about to say that. She rose to her feet, coming face-to-face with Brandon again. "Cline is an unusual name."

"It's for Patsy. She's my favorite singer." He smiled again. He had straight white teeth and a jawline to die for. "So I figured Cline was the way to go."

She forced a smile. She had a gap between her two front teeth. Some people thought it was trendy, considering the models who'd become famous for flaunting theirs. But Mary wasn't model material. At five-three, with natural red hair and a light dusting of freckles, she was only mildly pretty. Her sister disagreed. She insisted that Mary was the ultimate girl next door, created for secret male fantasy. Of course, Alice had a vivid imagination. In fact, it was Alice who'd concocted this seduction plan. Mary never would've hatched it by herself. She wasn't a femme fatale. She wasn't even sure how she was going to get Brandon interested in her.

Before she got lost in anxiety, she returned to their discussion. "I like some of Patsy Cline's songs. My grandmother used to listen to her." Her mother used to play those old records, too. Mama loved Patsy's music. But she was being cautious not to bring Mama into this.

Brandon knitted his eyebrows. Suddenly he was looking at her in a troubled way. Then he asked, "Do you know who I am?"

Good God. Mary struggled to maintain her composure, but all she could muster was a dumbfounded blink. Why was he being suspicious of her? Was it his lawyer's instincts, his ability to sniff out liars? Even Cline was cocking his head, taking a cue from his master.

Determined to hang tough, she found the phony will to say, "I'm sorry. But am I supposed to know who you are?" She quickly added, "Are you a politician or something?"

A light breeze stirred his hair. He wore it combed straight back, expertly cut and groomed. "Is that what I look like to you?"

"Sort of. But it was just a guess." She was still worried about why he suspected her of knowing his identity. Nonetheless, she spoke casually. "So are you going to tell me who you are?"

He shrugged. "I come from a famous family."

"You're not related to the Kennedys, are you?" She stayed on the political vein, trying not to veer too far from what was supposed to be her first impression of him. "A nephew? A cousin?"

"No, it's nothing like that. I'm Brandon Talbot. I'm an entertainment lawyer, and my brother and father are country musicians. Tommy and Kirby Talbot."

"Oh, wow." She acted surprised. "You're related to Tommy Talbot?" It was easier directing the conversation toward him. Tommy wasn't part of the ordeal with her mom. "He's superfamous, especially in this town."

"And my father is considered a legend." He laughed a little. "Sometimes he'll even be the first to say it."

Dang, she thought. He was making jokes about his dad's ego, and her mind was drifting back to the past, to that fateful summer, eight long years ago, when Mama had taken a trip to Nashville hoping to become a published songwriter.

Lo and behold, the almighty Kirby had noticed her peddling her songs around town. And while he was charming her into bed, he promised to buy them. After their short-lived affair ended, he ghosted her. Mama returned to Oklahoma feeling like a tramp and a failure. Only she hadn't given up. She'd continued to reach out to Kirby, trying to get him to make good on his promise. He'd treated her like a crazed fan instead, even filing a restraining order against her, which was where Brandon came into it. He was the attorney who'd drafted the order, making Mama out to be a stalker.

Nothing was ever the same again, and no matter how hard Mary had tried to hold her family together, it didn't work. Mama spiraled into a horrible depression, and Alice became a moody child who eventually grew into a rebellious teenager. Mostly, though, what Alice wanted was to get back at Kirby, and Mary vowed that someday she would help her do it. So after Mama died this year, they'd put their plan into action.

Initially they considered suing Kirby, but since they didn't have any proof that he had promised to buy their mother's songs, it didn't seem like a viable option. But taking it to the court of public opinion did. They decided that they could sell their story to a celebrity gossip site and expose Kirby for the bastard that he was. They changed their minds when Kirby's brand-new biography hit the stands. Once they read the book, they discovered that it was filled with scandalous tales, far juicer than anything they could tell the press.

Alice concocted a new plan that involved Brandon. From what she uncovered, some of his friends on social media commented that he needed to find "a nice girl" and settle down. Mary assumed the remarks were made in jest. But Alice believed it was an avenue worth pursuing. If Brandon was becoming intrigued with everyday girls instead of the socialites who were typically draped on his arm, Mary could win him over. Then, once he was hooked, she could dump him, the way his dad had done to their mom. Afterward, they could contact Kirby and tell him who they were and why they'd duped Brandon, teaching both father and son a lesson.

And now here Mary was, looking into Brandon's vast blue eyes and trying not to drown in them.

She blinked and said, "Doesn't your dad have a biography that was just released?" She tried to sound uncertain. But damn if her heart wasn't pounding again. "I seem to recall hearing something about it. Or am I mixing him up with another country star?"

"No, you definitely heard right." He patted Cline's head when the dog turned to look at a boat that went by. "It's making all kinds of buzz. The bestseller lists, too."

She downplayed her interest in it. "I get most of my books from the library. Or the classics, anyway. I like to read those in hardcover." She shifted her bag for effect, letting him know there was timeless literature inside. "Otherwise, I use an ereader." She hesitated before she asked, "Did you think I was a fan, trying to talk to you because of your family?"

He nodded. "That happens to me a lot. And it's gotten worse since Dad's book came out. But mostly it's Matt who's been bearing the brunt of it. He's our half brother in Texas. He was Dad's secret kid when we were growing up."

She'd read about how horribly Kirby had treated Matt. Kirby hadn't been a particularly good parent to Brandon or Tommy, either. He'd been drunk or stoned for most of their lives. Supposedly he was clean and sober now. But according to the book, even when Kirby was at his worst, Brandon had a favorable relationship with him—unlike his brothers, who'd butted heads with their dad. These days they were working on being one big happy family. She couldn't imagine what that was like. Mama had lost her zest for living long before she'd died.

"Who are you?" Brandon asked.

Mary started. "I'm sorry. What?"

"Your name, what you do for a living."

"Oh, right." She needed to stop being so jumpy around him. "I'm Mary McKenzie." She didn't have to worry about her last name ringing a bell with him. It was different from her mother's. "I work at Sugar Sal's. It's a specialty bakery."

"I've heard of that place, but I've never been there. I do have a sweet tooth, though. It's one of my vices."

She didn't want to think about what his other vices might be. "I've only worked there for three months. I worked at a bakery in Oklahoma City, too."

"Is that where you're from?"

"Yes." She wasn't going to trip herself up by pretending to be from somewhere else. Lots of people were from Oklahoma City, not just the woman he and his father had trashed. "I'm just settling into Nashville."

He smiled his perfect smile. "Well, welcome to Music City. What brought you here?"

If he only knew, she thought. But she had a ready-made answer. She and Alice had concocted a story ahead of time. "My sister met a guy online. He's from Tennessee, and they started a long-distance relationship. She moved here to be near him, but it didn't work out. Alice is only nineteen, and she's already had a slew of boyfriends." That part was true. Alice thrived on male attention.

"That explains why your sister came here, but what about you?"

"I needed a change of scenery." She wished he wasn't staring so intently at her. His eyes were unnerving. The dog was staring at her, too. To keep her words flowing, she prattled on. "I'm a pastry assistant, but I've been taking continuing education courses to become a certified pastry chef. I'm almost done, so now I'm trying to help Alice figure out what she should do."

"Where do her interests lie?"

"She hasn't made up her mind, but she's leaning toward something in fashion. Design, maybe. She'll be starting community college in the fall. She can be a bit flighty, so I hope she sticks with it." Mary wasn't going to lie about her sister's personality. If Brandon ever met her, he would see it for himself. "Sometimes I worry about how much time she spends online and her penchant for partying. I convinced her to delete her accounts when we moved here. I wanted her to have a clean slate, but that didn't last very long. She opened new ones and started partying with new people here." In actuality, Alice had deleted her old pages to erase her former presence online and make her and Mary's past less traceable. But Alice's social life was still wilder than it should be.

Brandon nodded as if he understood. Then he said, "I know what it's like to worry about a sibling. Tommy used to be flighty, too. Mostly it was his daredevil ways that scared me."

"It's tough to say what will happen with Alice. Maybe she'll become a successful designer someday. She's actually pretty talented in that regard. She just needs to learn to apply herself."

"I'm familiar with the fashion industry. My mother used to be a model. She runs a beauty products empire now. Her name is Melinda Miller."

"She's your mom?" Mary feigned ignorance, pretending not to know who Kirby's ex-wife was. "I've seen her infomercials on TV. Gosh, you really are from a famous family." She made a joke. "Not quite the Kennedys, but…"

He laughed at her silly attempt at humor.

A second later, they both went silent. In the next awkward moment, she searched for something to say.

She finally murmured, "I hope it doesn't seem weird that I told you so much about my sister, about how troubled she is and her boyfriends and whatnot. I'm not usually so open with strangers."

"Me, neither. We've certainly covered a lot of ground." He sent her a teasing wink. "But I think I'd rather hear about your boyfriends."

Mary's cheeks turned hot. He was flirting, and she was standing there like an imbecile. Should she tell him that she was single? Well, of course she should. The whole point was to get together with him if she could.

She went for the truth, letting it sputter off her tongue. "My love life isn't very exciting. I'm twenty-five, and as far as actual boyfriends go, there's only been one significant relationship. And even he didn't matter as much as he should have."

Brandon moved closer to her. "You're still young. You've got plenty of time to meet someone who matters. Now, me? I'll be thirty-seven this year."

"I'll bet you've had lots of girlfriends." She already knew that he did. His online profiles were filled with beautiful women.

He shrugged. "I've had my fair share, but not like Tommy. Women used to throw themselves at him. He's married now, with a baby on the way. It's the happiest he's ever been."

"That's good." She'd read about Tommy and his wife, Sophie, in the book. Matt's relationship with his fiancée, Libby, was showcased, too. Libby was also the author of the book, the biographer Kirby had hired to tell his story. "I guess entertainment lawyers don't have groupies, then?"

"No, I can't say that we do." He moved closer still. "But it's an intriguing idea."

Mary's throat went tight. With the "intrigued" way he was looking at her, you'd think he was picturing her as his sweet little groupie. She could actually feel the air growing thick between them. And now her mixed-up mind was running rampant, and she was imagining what kind of lover he would be.

A powerful one, she thought, who would make her sigh and melt and moan—right at his feet.

Panic set in. "I should let you go." She was overwhelmed by the hunger, the heat, the dizzying urge to share his bed. "You came here to walk Cline, and I'm taking up all of your time." Before she blew it completely, she added, "Maybe I'll run into you next Sunday." She was supposed to be setting a honey trap, not darting off like a scared rabbit.

"Sure. I'd like that." He spoke softly, fluidly, as smooth as the Tennessee whiskey he probably drank. "I'd like it very much."

"Me, too." Her heart pounded unmercifully inside her chest. She'd just caught a whiff of his summer-fresh cologne. Or maybe it was the scent of a finely milled soap lingering on his skin.

"I'll be here, same place, same time." He rattled his dog's leash. "Same husky."

"Okay." She cursed her pounding heart. She'd captured his interest, doing what she'd set out to do.

But for now, she needed to escape with her emotions intact. "Bye, Brandon."

"Goodbye, Mary."

She walked away, doing her best to stay calm. But even as she departed she sensed that he'd spun around to watch her, as aroused by her as she was by him.

As soon as Mary entered their apartment, her sister rushed to greet her. "What happened? Did you talk to him?"

"Yes." And she was still trying to get a handle on the lust-tinged way he made her feel. She removed her sweater and draped it over a dining chair. "I was so nervous I don't know how I got through it."

"You have to tell me everything." Alice grabbed her hand and dragged her toward the sofa.

They sat side by side. Thank goodness the sliding glass door to their itty-bitty patio was open. Mary needed the air.

"So?" Alice pressed.

"Can I have a minute? I need to catch my breath."

"But I've been waiting here for hours."

"All I'm asking for is a minute."

"Whatever." Alice rolled her heavily lined eyes. She went through phases, and currently she was on a cowpunk kick, where she'd patterned her style after a vintage trend derived from cowboy and punk rock influences. At the moment, she wore a skintight Western ensemble and gothic jewelry. Her bleached platinum hair was short and spiked. But no matter how outlandish she looked, her beauty remained evident. Mama had been gorgeous, too. Mary had always been plain by comparison. Yet she was the one who'd just had an encounter with Kirby's devastatingly handsome son.

"Time's up," Alice said. She pointed to the clock on the cable TV box. "It's been at least a minute."

If Mary wasn't so frazzled, she would have laughed. Her sister was one of the most impatient people she knew.

She started with saying, "He seemed to like me." Just thinking about him was making her breathe harder and faster. "He's even more striking up close. It was different than checking out his pictures or spying on him from a distance. Looking into his eyes was just so…real, I guess."

"So he's hotter than you anticipated? And he seemed to like you?" Alice waggled her brows suggestively. "You shouldn't have any trouble getting him into bed."

"I'm not…" Mary frowned, steeped in her own forbidden desires. "I already told you that even if he took an interest in me, sex was off the table. I couldn't possibly—"

"You're such a prude." Alice shook her head. "But you'll just have to hold his attention in other ways." She leaned forward. "So tell me the rest of it."

Mary expounded on the beginning of their conversation, before she'd started fantasizing about being his lover.

Alice listened and said, "I'll bet you were really scared when he asked you if you knew who he was."

"I was petrified." So afraid he'd figured her out.

"It sounds like you handled it just fine. I knew you'd be a natural at presenting yourself as a nice girl."

"It didn't make me feel very nice." For now, she just felt confused. "What if we have him pegged wrong? What if he isn't responsible for what happened? He might not have even known that his dad was lying about our mom. If he filed the restraining order because he believed that Mama was a stalker, then he was just doing his job."

Alice gaped at her. "You can't be serious."

She hated to think of Brandon as a bad person now that she'd met him. Or maybe she just hated to think of herself being attracted to someone so cold and calculating. "I'm just covering all of the bases."

"Come on, Mar. Don't make him out to be innocent in all of this. Attorneys are known for being shrewd."

"I just want to be sure, that's all."

"I don't have any doubts, and I guarantee when it's over, you'll be convinced that he's as ruthless as his dad."

"You're probably right." But now that the wheels were in motion, she needed to figure him out, to know for certain. "At least I'll be seeing him next week."

"You should bring him some pastries. You can bake something special just for him." Alice waggled her eyebrows again. "A little sugar to tempt his palate."

"He did say that he had a sweet tooth. But I'll have to think about what to make." She had no idea what his preferences would be. "I should bake some doggy biscuits for Cline, too."

"Oh, that's perfect. It's exactly what a nice girl would do. Bring extra treats for that blue-eyed beast of his."

Mary jumped to the husky's defense. "Cline isn't a beast. He seemed really gentle."

"Maybe so, but that doesn't make his master a good guy." Alice frowned, her distain for Brandon obvious. "If he falls for you, I wonder if he'll post pictures of you on his Instagram. Or maybe selfies of you and him and the dog."

Mary didn't want to think that far ahead. Yet she couldn't help but recall how intensely both Brandon and Cline had stared at her. "In person their eyes are almost the same color."

Alice squinted. "It's too bad you're not going to seduce him all the way. Sex would make the revenge that much sweeter."

"Not for me." She feared that sleeping with him would be dangerous to her soul. Not just because of the way he made her feel, but because of her charade, too. "That would be carrying it too far."

"Okay, so you've got your morals. But it's not as if you're a virgin or anything."

"That's not the point." Her sex life wasn't the issue. Or her lack thereof, she thought. She'd slept

with only one guy: the boyfriend who'd barely mattered. "Brandon isn't my type, anyway."

"I didn't know you had a type."

"Well, if I did, it wouldn't be with a lawyer who
might dominate me."

Her sister looked stunned. "Oh, my God. Did he
say something kinky to you?"

"What? No. I didn't mean it like that." She tried
to explain, without admitting how deeply he aroused
her. "He just seems as if he'd be as powerful in the
bedroom as he is in the courtroom, or wherever he
does his best work."

"That's quite an observation." Alice leaned back
on their floral-printed sofa—the one they'd bought
during her boho phase—and lifted her booted feet
onto the coffee table. "And seriously, who are you
trying to kid? You totally want to shag him."

"Can we change the subject, please?" Mary
couldn't bear to sit here and listen to this.

"Well, I'm all for it. As long as you make him suffer once it's over."

What part of changing the subject didn't her sister
understand? "I don't want to keep talking about this."

Alice readjusted her position, lowering her feet
to the floor. "You brought up the domination stuff,
not me."

"And you're making a bigger deal out of it than
it is."

"All right, but no matter how attracted to him you
are, just remember that we're doing this for Mama.
So whatever you do, don't fall for him for real."

"I would never do that." Mary knew better than to develop feelings for a man she didn't even know if she could trust.

Two

On Friday night, Brandon rode in the back of a limo with his date by his side, wondering how many black-tie events he'd attended over the course of his life. Hundreds? Thousands? At the moment, it seemed like millions.

He was bored already, and they hadn't even arrived at the hotel. He served on the committee that was hosting the party. He cared deeply about his charity work, but how many luxurious dinners and big, sweeping dances could he stand?

The real problem, he decided, was that he couldn't get the redhead he'd met at the park out of his mind. Mary McKenzie. So wholesome, so cute, so all-American and average. He doubted that she'd ever worn a glittering gown or been to a fancy ball.

"Are you all right?" Doreen asked. She was one of his occasional lovers—a long, leggy brunette and twice-divorced heiress who relied on a carb-free diet to maintain her figure and Botox to keep her frown lines at bay. Tonight she was wearing a set of spidery lashes. Brandon had gotten used to seeing her in them, but he'd never quite grasped the point. He couldn't imagine gluing something onto his eyelids.

"I'm fine," he said.

"You seem distracted to me."

"I'm just sitting here." And thinking about seeing Mary again—a fresh-faced twenty-five-year-old who worked at a bakery. She was so damned different from his norm. He frowned at Doreen. "Do you ever get tired of the same ol'?"

She gave him a pointed look. "See, I knew something was going on with you."

"Maybe I'm just going through a midlife crisis and wanting things I shouldn't have." That might account for him obsessing about a woman he barely knew.

She turned on the light above their heads. "Did you meet someone who's got your boxers in a bunch?"

He flinched as if he'd been kicked. "What?"

She raised her delicately arched eyebrows. "You did, didn't you?"

His stomach clenched. He'd just gotten called out by a savvy socialite. "You don't know what you're talking about."

"Oh, believe me, I do. A woman knows when a man has another female on his mind."

"There's no one." He wasn't about to admit that he couldn't wait to return to the park on Sunday and reunite with a stranger who made his skin hot. He couldn't remember the last time anyone made him feel that way. He'd been on autopilot for so long, he hadn't noticed until now.

Doreen sighed. "It doesn't matter to me if you want someone else. Because I do, too."

He turned suspicious. Was she making up stories to try to con the truth out of him? "If you're mooning over another man, then why are you here with me?"

She removed a gilded compact from her clutch. "You and I made these plans a long time ago. And since we haven't been together for months, I figured we were just here as friends."

That was a fair assumption, he supposed. It wasn't just her that he hadn't been with in a while. He hadn't slept with anyone in what seemed like forever. And he didn't want to, either, until Mary had come along.

Doreen opened the mirror and checked her appearance. "The man I'm hoping to nab is going to be at this party, so I thought—"

"You'd use me to get his attention?" If Brandon gave a crap, he would be mad. But he didn't care if she was after another guy. It didn't matter. "Who is he?"

"David Norton."

"The retail billionaire?" He should have known she would aim high. "Wasn't he just named as one of the richest people in the States? He came in at number twelve, as I recall."

She made a duck face, posing as if the compact was a camera. "He was number nine, actually, but who's counting?"

"You are, obviously."

She closed the mirror and tucked it back into her clutch. "I don't need his money. I have plenty of my own."

That was true. Between her inheritance and her ex-husbands, she was set for life. "Yeah, okay, but isn't he a little old for you?" David Norton was a good person, a charitable man, but he was also pushing seventy. Doreen was all of forty.

"He appreciates women my age. And in our social circle, that's saying a lot. Do you know how many twentysomethings have stolen my lovers away from me? I'll bet the gal who caught your eye is a sweet young thing."

Maybe too sweet, he thought. Tigresses like Doreen were more his style.

She snared his gaze. "Is your new love interest going to be at this soiree?"

"She isn't—" He stopped and cursed. He'd just more or less admitted that there was another woman on his mind.

"She isn't what?" Doreen pressured him to come clean.

He went ahead and said it. "She isn't part of this crowd."

"Oh, my." Placing a dramatic hand against the

jeweled bodice of her gown, she gave a ladylike gasp. "You're stepping outside of your regal realm? That spells trouble to me."

He hated it when she mocked him. Sometimes she even called him the King of Nashville High Society. "Knock it off."

"I'm serious, Brandon. Those types of hookups don't work."

"I never said I was getting together with her." Sure, he wanted to, but the only thing they'd agreed on was another run-in at the park. Nonetheless, Mary had seemed leery of him. He could tell that he'd made her nervous. "I don't want to talk about her, anyway." He preferred to keep his distorted hunger to himself. "Let's just get this night over with so you can land a date with David."

Doreen's pouty pink lips tilted into a smile. "You're going to help me with that?"

"Sure. Why not?" He turned off the overhead light that she'd left on. For now, the only thing he wanted was for Sunday morning to roll around so he could see Mary again.

Mary parked her car on a side street and walked to the park, wishing she didn't have to figure Brandon out. It would be easier if she was convinced, the way Alice was, that he was a bad person. But for now, she wasn't sure of anything.

She adjusted the insulated tote bag on her arm. She'd baked a variety of pastries. She'd also brought a thermos of medium roast coffee, and cups and plates and everything else they would need. She was good at packing picnics. Or whatever this makeshift breakfast was going to be.

As she cut across the grass, she searched for Brandon. When she spotted him, her heart jumped to her throat. She continued toward him. By now, he'd seen her, as well, and was heading in her direction with the dog by his side. It was warmer this morning than it had been last week. In keeping with the weather, he was wearing khaki shorts and a pale green T-shirt. But no matter how casually he was dressed, he looked as if he'd just stepped out of the pages of a men's fashion magazine. He'd obviously gotten his sense of style from his mother. His father always looked like an outlaw, draped in shades of black.

As they got closer, Brandon smiled at her with a quick flash of those perfect white teeth. A shadowy chill ran through her, as if she was about to be bitten by a tall, tanned, play-in-the-daylight vampire. A man with no soul? Or just a man with too much sex appeal? Either way, she sucked it up—no pun intended—and returned his smile.

"Hey, Mary," he said, as they stood face-to-face.

"Hi." She adjusted the bag on her arm. "I didn't bring a book today. I brought goodies for you and Cline instead."

Brandon seemed surprised. Apparently the possibility of her baking for him hadn't crossed his mind.

"What kind of goodies?" he asked.

"For you, I made raspberry-and-ginger muffins, chocolate-and-cinnamon scones and crisp apple fritters. For Cline, I whipped up a batch of peanut butter, bacon and pumpkin treats."

"That's so sweet of you." He moistened his lips. "Can we try them now?"

"Definitely." She hesitated. "I brought coffee, too, just in case." He'd mentioned on social media that he was a coffee drinker, but she was pretending to be unsure. She was also trying not to fixate on his mouth.

He gestured to a nearby picnic bench. "Shall we?"

She nodded and warned herself to get a grip. Fixating on his mouth wasn't part of today's game plan.

They sat across from each other, and she was grateful for the tabletop between them. Although Brandon dropped Cline's leash, the loyal husky didn't leave his master's side.

Mary set everything up, making it look as pretty as possible. Presentation was part of her job. She poured the coffee and gave him his. "Cream or sugar?"

"Two creams." He held up two fingers.

She handed him the little packets, along with a stir stick. "I do sugar." She sweetened her coffee while he lightened his. "These are Cline's, obviously." She slid a Baggie of the bone-shaped biscuits across the table. "If you want to give him one."

"You can do the honors." He moved them back over to her. "Just call him around to your side and ask him to 'sit up.' That will get him begging for you."

She followed Brandon's instructions, and in no time, Cline was sitting up with his nose twitching.

She dropped a biscuit, and he caught it. The husky reclined next to her to gobble it up. She returned her attention to his master. "I think I just made a friend for life."

"Can't say as I blame him." Brandon looked at her as if she was as tempting as the pastries she'd brought. "Which of these should I try first?"

"That's up to you." As a flame ignited in her belly, she sipped her coffee and wondered if she should have brought iced water instead. At least she could have cooled herself off with it.

He reached for a chocolate-and-cinnamon scone. It was gooiest of the three, with its thick, creamy icing. She watched as he took a big masculine bite.

He swallowed and said, "Damn, this is good."

"Thank you. I'm glad you like it." She noticed that there was graffiti on his side of the table: an old-fashioned heart with initials inside it. There were dirty words scratched onto the surface, too. Nothing was ever as innocent as it seemed, not even Mary. If Brandon knew what she up to, he would be throwing the pastries back in her face.

"Are you going to join me?" he asked.

Anxious to clear her thoughts, she put a raspberry muffin on a paper plate. "I'll have this. But you can take home whatever we don't eat." She'd packed enough for seconds and thirds.

"I'd be happy to." He drank his coffee. "When I was a kid, I had a nanny named Fleur, and she used to sneak me extra cookies. She said it was because I was always so well-behaved and she thought I should be rewarded for it."

"Did she help raise you?" Mary couldn't have imagined someone aside from her mother kissing her forehead, or giving her cookies or tucking her in at night.

He shook his head. "She wasn't around for very long. I had lots of nannies. But she's the most memorable to me. I was about seven or eight then. I think she left to go back to the Netherlands. I had the craziest crush on her." He smiled. "My first crush and it was all because of those cookies."

She tried to picture him as a child. But all she saw was the polished man sitting across from her. "Were they chocolate chip?"

"I don't remember, but they probably were." He toasted her with his next bite. The scone he was eating had chocolate chips in it. "So who was yours?"

She picked at her muffin, breaking off crusty little pieces. "My what?"

"First crush."

"Oh, right." She had an unwelcome crush on him. That was for darn sure. She could barely focus on her answer. But she searched her memories and said, "In middle school. An older boy named Kasey. But he never liked me back."

Brandon stared across the table at her. "He would probably like you now."

Her pulse dipped and dived. "I got over him a long time ago."

His stare got deeper, more intense. "I kept thinking about you all week. I couldn't get you off my mind."

She tried to keep things light, to fight the sexual feelings he incited. "About me being a new Nashville resident?"

"About everything, I guess. I'd really like to take you out, Mary."

Oh wow. He'd just asked her on a real live date. Things were moving faster than she expected. But she couldn't turn him down, not if she wanted to get to know him better.

"Where would we go?" she managed to ask.

He smiled. "Someplace nice."

For the *nice* girl she was supposed to be? The thought made her breath rush out. "I'm not used to fancy places."

"It doesn't have to be fancy. We can do cozy." He paused and added, "With a good-night kiss."

She panicked. "What if I decide that we shouldn't kiss on the first date?"

"Then I'll be forced to wait until the next time I see you." He finished his scone, swallowing the last glazed bite. "But I hope that doesn't happen. What man in his right mind wouldn't want to kiss you?"

He wasn't just any man, she thought. He was the attorney who'd filed a restraining order against her mother. "You're making my head spin."

He frowned. "Why do I make you so uncomfortable? What am I doing wrong?"

"Nothing." He'd already done it years ago. "I just haven't been on a date in a while."

"That's okay. I'll bring you up to speed. Do you like Chinese food? I can get us a private booth at the Crystal Buddha."

"That sounds good." She toyed with her napkin. "I've never been there, but I've heard rave reviews about it."

"How about Thursday night?"

"That's fine. I'll give you my number and you can text me when you make the reservation. Maybe you should give me your number now, too."

After they completed the exchange, he glanced past her and said, "I guess we're boring my dog."

She followed his line of sight. Cline was sprawled out on the grass, fast asleep. "Maybe he needs his own date."

"I think he's content just the way he is."

She nodded. The husky didn't seem to have a care in the world. In the next quiet instant, she asked, "Would you be okay with me buying your dad's biography? I'm getting curious to read it."

He angled his head. "Really? Why?"

"To learn more about your family and how you fit in with them." And because she could discuss the book with him and get his reactions. "It might make for an interesting conversation when we go out."

"Sure, we can talk about it over dinner. It would probably be better if you knew my background, anyway, with how public it is. But you'd better read fast because it's four hundred pages."

"I'll do my best." She couldn't tell him that she'd already read it several times.

"Too bad there isn't a book about your family and how you fit in with them. I'm going to have to learn about you the normal way."

Mary merely nodded. Normal didn't exist in this farce of a situation. But she had to protect herself. Her and Alice and Mama. "I'm just a regular person from a regular family."

"We're going to make a strange pair. You and me."

"The strangest," she agreed, praying that she could handle their date—and the kiss that loomed between them.

After work, when Brandon came home from the office to his downtown loft, Tommy made an impromptu visit. Brandon also owned an estate near their dad's house, but this was his main residence.

Tommy entered the loft like the country superstar he was, decked out in fancy Western wear, with his light brown hair loosely tousled. He had hazel eyes and features similar to their father. Brandon resembled their mom, except that his hair was black and hers was blond. Their parents had gotten divorced ages ago, but Mom had forgiven Dad for his indiscretions, and they'd become friends again.

"What's going on?" Brandon asked.

"I had a meeting in the area and thought I'd stop by."

"Was it with the producers of the show?" His brother had signed a megadeal to appear on *Music Mentors*, a popular reality show on a major network.

"Yep. We'll be filming soon." Tommy moved farther into the loft. "As long as I'm here, I was wondering if you'd want to have dinner with Sophie and me?" He patted his stomach. "Chef has been trying to fatten me up. You know, so my pregnant wife doesn't feel bad."

As far as Brandon could tell, the father-to-be hadn't gained an ounce. But the last time he'd seen Sophie, she was beautifully round. "I appreciate the offer, but I'm going out this evening." Brandon strode to the bar to pour his brother a glass of sparkling berry-flavored water. Tommy never drank alcohol. Growing up with an alcoholic father had turned him off to it. Brandon drank in moderation, a cocktail here and there, a glass of wine with a meal. He didn't have an addictive personality. But their old man sure did.

He handed Tommy the water.

"Thanks." His brother took a swig. "Where are you going tonight?"

"I have a date." Brandon thought about Mary's natural red hair. Or he assumed it was natural. To him, it didn't look dyed. So far, he'd seen it only in a braid. He hoped that she wore it loose tonight. If she let him kiss her, he was going to do his damnedest to run his fingers through it. "She isn't my usual type, though."

Tommy looked at him curiously. "So what type is she?"

"She's a pastry chef assistant, but she's working toward getting her certification. She's originally from Oklahoma, shares an apartment with her younger sister and likes to read at the park. She seems sweet—you know, unassuming. I never even noticed her until she approached me about my dog."

"Really?" Tommy widened his eyes. "My aristocratic brother is going out with a commoner? Boy, would I love to be a fly on the wall to see that."

Brandon blew out a breath. "Why is everyone making such a fuss about me getting interested in someone from outside my social circle?"

"What do you mean, everyone? Who else knows about her?"

"I mentioned her to Doreen. She could tell that I'd met someone. But I encouraged her to go after David Norton, anyway." When Tommy gave him a blank look, he added, "The retail billionaire who just opened the new cancer research center here."

"Oh, yeah. That guy. I can see Doreen with him. But you with someone who approached you at the park?" his brother teased. "Now that's epic."

"I don't know. Maybe it is." Brandon glanced around his loft, wondering what Mary would think of his place. He collected modern and contemporary art, and he'd just acquired a trio of abstract nudes he'd hung in his bedroom. They were erotic in nature, and he'd never bought anything like that before. But after he'd met Mary, he'd felt compelled to have them. The way he felt compelled to have her, too?

"So what's the difference this time?" Tommy asked.

Still lost in thought, Brandon frowned. "What?"

"Why are you interested in someone like this?"

He thought about the paintings again. "It might just be sexual."

Tommy finished his water and put the empty glass down. "You're having fantasies about a good girl."

"Yeah, and it makes me feel like a shark." A predator circling for blood. "Hell, I shouldn't even be telling you this."

His brother didn't seem concerned. "At least you're opening up your horizons."

And lusting after a woman who'd had only one boyfriend to speak of? Maybe he shouldn't try to kiss her tonight. Maybe he shouldn't even plan on seeing her again after this. "She hardly knew anything about our family when I first met her. But she asked me if I wouldn't mind if she read Dad's book. I told her it would be okay, so she's supposed to finish reading it before our date."

Tommy scoffed. "Did you warn her about what a jerk our father can be?"

"He's not a jerk anymore." Their dad was trying to make amends for his wrongdoings, for all the times he'd lied to their mother, or ignored him and Tommy or left Matt out in the cold.

His brother squinted. "It's amazing how you never fought with him, not once."

Because Brandon was the son who'd behaved, the one who never caused any trouble. The peacekeeper, as the family liked to point out. Tommy had been trouble on wheels. And Matt? His only crime was being born on the wrong side of the blanket. Dad had hurt a lot of people, but he was different now.

"I'm going to take off," Tommy said. "Have fun on your date, and bring your new lady friend around sometime if you two become an item. I'd love to meet her."

"It's just one night. One dinner." After that, he didn't know what he was doing. "I'm not even picking her up at her apartment. She wants to meet me at the restaurant."

"She sounds independent."

More like cautious, Brandon thought. He changed the subject, letting Tommy get out the door. "Give Sophie a hug from me."

"Will do."

He watched his brother leave. Tommy had married his dearest childhood friend. Initially he was only supposed to be her baby's sperm donor. But during the course of their arrangement, they'd fallen in love.

Brandon had never come remotely close to being in love. Nor did he see it happening to him. Of course, that's what Tommy used to say, too. They'd grown up in a mixed-up situation, where love and marriage never made much sense. Yet in spite of that, both his brothers were creating warm and stable families of their own. So maybe Brandon was wrong about his future, and the possibility existed for him, too.

He shook away the thought and went into his bathroom to take a shower and get ready to see Mary. This was definitely not the time to think about love. Or sex, he reminded himself. He needed to get through this date with a suppressed libido and a clear head.

Three

*O*ne. *Two. Three.*

Mary stood at the bathroom sink, counting her breaths. She remembered Mama doing that whenever she was getting ready for a big event.

Four. Five. Six.

She frowned into the mirror. Mama's old method wasn't working. Mary was still apprehensive about her date with Brandon.

Her sister came into the room, and her reflection appeared behind Mary's, like a hitchhiking ghost. It even gave her a chill. When Alice was little, she used to bug Mary to read ghost stories to her.

"You look really pretty," Alice said.

Mary washed her mind of ghosts. "I do?"

Her sister nodded. "Your hair looks like Mama's."

"I scrunched it with some mousse." But she hadn't done it to emulate their mother. "Her hair was a darker shade of red than mine."

"It still reminds me of those old pictures of her, the ones from before."

Before Kirby Talbot had ruined her, Mary thought. She understood exactly what her sister meant.

Alice sighed. "It's not fair."

"I know." Mama had died of heart failure at just fifty-two years old. "She got a raw deal, first with losing our dad, then with Kirby taking advantage of her."

Alice's expression was tight. "I don't understand why our parents never got married."

"Because Dad didn't want to."

"Yeah, but it was like they were married, anyway. They lived together and had two kids. So what's the difference?"

"I can't speak for Dad or why he didn't think it was necessary. I only have scattered memories of him. And you don't remember him at all." Joel McKenzie was a long-distance truck driver who'd spent months at a time away from home. Then almost a year after Alice was born, he was in an accident that took his life. "He was good to Mama, though. She said that he was, even if he didn't want to get married."

"I think things would have been okay if he'd lived."

Mary nodded. "Mama never would have gone to Nashville or slept with Kirby if Dad had been around." She never would have been with Kirby if he'd been married at the time, either. She just wasn't that kind of person.

Alice sighed. "I miss her."

"Me, too." There wasn't a day that went by that Mary didn't long for their mom. They'd lost her six lonely months ago.

They both fell silent, a huge cloud of sorrow hanging between them. Then Alice said, "I don't know what I would have done if you hadn't been there to help pick up the pieces when Mama got so depressed. You were the one who used to pack my lunches and help me with my homework. Mama could barely get herself back and forth to work every day."

"It was a tough time for all of us." Mary considered the emotional state she and her sister were in now: the anger, the grief, the pain, the emotional cocktail that had become far too familiar. "And we're still affected by it."

"Yes, but at least we're doing something about it."

"With me dating Brandon?" Her anxiety returned. "Is my makeup okay?" She'd used dark brown mascara and an apricot lipstick called Summer Mischief. Somehow the name seemed fitting.

"Maybe just a little more blush." Alice rummaged through the cosmetics on the counter. "I'll do it for you." She swiped the brush across Mary's cheeks, adding a touch more color. "Perfect."

"Will you help me decide what to wear?" Mary was still in her robe. "I laid a couple of things out on my bed, but I'm not sure which way to go."

"No problem. Let's check it out."

They proceeded to Mary's bedroom. Alice evaluated each outfit, then gave the collection a critical eye. "I have something that I think will work better. Hold on."

She darted off and came back carrying a swingy little peach-colored cocktail dress with a lace bodice. "I bought this when I was into pastels, but I never wore it. I think it'll look smashing on you."

They were the same size, but their styles were rarely interchangeable. "Are you sure the front of it won't be too daring? I'm not used to things like that. Besides, I'm supposed be a proper girl. I can't show up for my first date all sexy and such." She was having enough trouble with the urges Brandon brought out in her.

"It's just a bit of lace. There's nothing daring about that. And it's totally lined, so no one is going to see anything but the fabric underneath. Just try it, okay?"

"All right." Mary slipped on the dress and stood in front of her mirrored closet doors to get the full effect. "Oh, wow. This is nice."

"Told ya." Alice went into Mary's closet for a pair of nude pumps. "You can wear these with it."

"What purse do you think I should carry?" She might as well let her sister choose the whole ensemble.

"Let's see." Alice rummaged through the closet and uncovered a black evening bag with a gold chain strap. "This will do. You should add some hoop ear-rings, too. I have a pair that will sparkle through your hair."

Soon Mary was ready, with every accessory in place.

A second later, Alice said, "You're going to knock him dead."

Mary didn't reply. She just needed to get in her car and go, before she lost her nerve.

From the moment Mary entered the restaurant, Brandon couldn't take his eyes off her. And now, as they sat across from each other in a scarlet booth with a gold velvet curtain dividing them from the rest of the patrons, he was still staring at her. He thought she looked fresh and radiant, an unpretentious woman striking a complicated chord inside him.

Was his attraction to her primarily sexual? Was that what was driving him? Or was it something more? In the past, he always knew what he wanted from a woman. But with Mary, he was conflicted.

The orchid-and-candle centerpiece cast a soft glow, making the table seem like a gentle barrier, even if the wood was polished to a slick, hard shine.

While they drank hot tea and sampled appetizers, he waited to see if she was going to mention his father's book. So far, she hadn't brought it up. But they were still in the preliminary stages of their date. The small talk, he thought. The stuff he would prefer to get past.

He decided to broach the subject himself. He finished the pot sticker he'd been eating and said, "I'm dying to know if you read *Kirbyville*." That was the title of the biography, as well as the nickname for the luxurious compound where his dad still lived and where Brandon and Tommy had been raised.

"Yes, I read it. I devoured it, in fact." She hesitated, as if she was summoning her thoughts. "I'm fascinated that the author is Matt's fiancée. That they met while she was researching the book. I liked that she included a bit about her relationship with Matt in it and how they became a couple. It was nice that Tommy's relationship with Sophie was highlighted, too." She paused once again. "But the parts about you were the most interesting."

He studied her in the pale light. "Because I'm depicted as the levelheaded one? The glue that holds my family together?"

She reached for her tea, the jasmine brew steaming in its cup. "Is that what you are, Brandon?"

"It's who I've always been, I suppose." But at the moment, he didn't feel very levelheaded. Would she let him kiss her tonight? Would he be able to tangle his hands in her hair? She'd worn it long and loose, just as he'd hoped she would.

"There were portions of the book that I found unsettling," she said. "But I…"

He gauged her hesitation. "If you're concerned about bringing up sensitive subjects, don't be. Everything in Dad's biography is fair game. He's the one who put it out there, and as far as I'm concerned, you can say whatever you think."

"It's about your parents and their relationship." She scrunched up her freckled nose. "In the sections where your mom was interviewed, she said that she would have preferred a monogamous husband. But she allowed your dad to have mistresses because she knew he would have cheated anyway. I don't see where that benefited her."

"I know." He admitted how it affected him. "That was always hard for us kids to comprehend, too. I think it's what made Tommy into a playboy when he got older, and why it took him so long to realize that he loved Sophie. We didn't have conventional guidelines to follow. I'm still not sure if I'll ever settle down. Marriage has always scared me. But maybe I'll get over that someday." For now, he was just trying to come to terms with his attraction to Mary.

After another brief pause, she said, "The other part about your parents' relationship that troubled me was that the only thing your mom ever asked your dad not to do, he still did."

"Having a baby with someone else? Then being a crummy father to that kid, besides?" Brandon couldn't deny how selfishly his father had behaved in that regard. Matt had been born to Kirby's longest-lasting mistress—a woman in Texas who'd more or less raised Matt alone.

"I don't know if I could have forgiven your father if I was Matt."

"You seem like a forgiving person to me." He couldn't imagine her holding a grudge.

She glanced away, and there was an awkward lull between them. A second later, she returned her gaze to his and said, "In the book, I was rooting for your mom when she divorced your dad. She seems like a good person."

"She is. But deep down, I think my father is, too. He's genuinely sorry for all the pain he caused."

"That's what he kept saying in the book, but it's still a lot of hurt. Not just to your mom and Matt and his mom, but to you and Tommy, too."

"Actually, it wasn't as bad for me. He wasn't an ideal parent, that's for sure. But he didn't back me into an emotional corner the way he did with Tommy."

She frowned. "Why would he, as loyal as you've always been to him?"

Brandon frowned, too. "You don't approve of the way I support him?"

"I didn't mean..." She seemed flustered, as if she feared she'd said too much.

"It's okay." He let her off the hook. He'd told her to be honest with her feelings. "Maybe you can meet my dad sometime and see what you think of him in person."

Her teacup rattled when she picked it up. "Maybe we should just stick to the here and now."

Yeah, he thought, maybe they should. This was only their first date and already he was thinking of introducing her to his dad? "I guess that would be a little soon, especially after you just read his book. Tommy is interested in meeting you, though."

She blinked at him. "You told your brother about me?"

"I mentioned that I was going out with someone new." He couldn't tell her the rest of what he'd said about her. About how it might only be sexual. About how mixed up he was about her. If he had his way, he would take her back to his place tonight and strip her beautifully bare.

"Is Tommy interested in every new person you date?"

"No. But I told him how different you are from the women I usually go out with."

"Different how?"

"I described you as sweet and unassuming." He pictured her in his bed, wrapped in a sheet with her hair strewn across his pillow. He had all sorts of wayward images of her rattling around in his mind. "I hope you don't mind being described that way."

She studied him over the rim of her cup. "You can describe me however you want. But the way you look at me makes me feel wilder than I am."

Her admission went straight to his zipper. "Maybe you've just been tempering that side of yourself before now."

"But I've never noticed feeling this way before." She lowered her voice. "I think it's coming from you."

Brandon could've batted this subject around all

night, but the waiter arrived with their entrées, putting an end to it.

After their server left, they settled into their meals. They'd both ordered spicy dishes.

Neither of them spoke. They'd gone from an intimate conversation to nothing at all. He couldn't stop staring at her and wondering about the wild feelings she'd mentioned. But he didn't think it would be polite to bring it up again, not while they were struggling for something to say.

He gestured to her paper-wrapped chopsticks and asked, "Don't you like using those?" He noticed that she'd opted for a fork.

She quickly replied, "I've never gotten the hang of chopsticks."

"I can teach you. But it would be easier if I sat next to you." It was a good excuse to move over to her side of the booth, to sit beside her, to breathe her in. "Do you want to give it a try?"

"Okay. But if I drop some food on my lap, don't laugh at me."

"Don't worry." He got up from his seat. "I'd never do that." He scooted next to her, and they turned to face each other. In the next oddly romantic moment, he moved a strand of her hair away from her face. Then, feeling the need to explain, he said, "I was just trying to keep it from getting in the way."

"Maybe I should do it." She tucked both sides of her hair behind her ears. With an audible breath, she opened her chopsticks and broke them apart. Then she asked, "What's the right way to hold these?"

"Just do it lightly. If you grip them too hard, that's when you might drop your food or send something flying." He demonstrated with his chopsticks, placing them where they were supposed to go. He explained that the bottom chopstick remained stationary, while the index and middle finger did the lifting with the second one. "See?" He raised a piece of chicken from her plate and put it back down. "Now you try it."

She kept fumbling and losing her grip. He suspected that her nerves were coming into play, with him sitting so close to her. The sexual energy between them was palpable, as thick and spicy as the sauce on their food.

She said, "Your meal is going to get cold if you stay here and try to help me eat mine."

He leaned a little closer. "But you've almost got it."

"I do?" She locked gazes with him instead of glancing down at her food.

He stared at her, too. "Just try it one more time."

She gave it another go, lifting a piece of diced bell pepper to her mouth. He watched her. She tried for another bite and missed her mark.

She shook her head. "At this rate, we'll be here all night."

That would be one way of spending the night with her, he supposed. "Just keep practicing when you can."

"I will. And thank you for trying to teach me."

She swapped the chopsticks for her fork. "But I think I'd better go back to this."

"No problem." He returned to his seat. The lesson was fun while it lasted.

"Where were we?" she asked.

He resumed eating. "What do you mean?"

"In my review of your father's biography."

"Maybe we should cover that another time." He wanted to learn more about her. "Why don't you tell me what the future holds for you?" He'd already admitted that he wasn't sure if he was ever going to settle down. "Do you plan on getting married someday?"

"I don't know." She heaved a sigh. "I'm probably as uncertain about it as you are."

"Really?" He expected a more conventional answer from her. "Why?"

"It just seems counterproductive to be waiting around for happily-ever-after."

Happily-ever-after aside, he still wanted to kiss her. That desire hadn't gone away. No matter how conflicted he was about her, he kept coming back to that damnable kiss. "Are your parents divorced, too? Is that why you're not any more marriage-minded than I am?" It seemed like a possibility to him, but he was still eager to see what her reasoning was.

She stirred the rest of the kung pao chicken on her plate. "My parents passed away, and I'd prefer not to talk about them. My grandmother is gone, too. Alice is my only family."

"I'm so sorry." He met her fractured gaze. Her

eyes were big and brown and sad. He could see her vulnerability from where he sat. "I had no idea it was just you and your sister." His family was quite literally an open book. But hers wasn't, and he needed to respect that. But the less he knew, the less she shared, the more of a mystery she became.

A mystery he didn't have a clue how to solve.

After Mary and Brandon finished their entrées, they ordered fried ice cream for dessert. While they waited for it to be served, she wished this were just a normal date where she didn't have to keep so much of herself hidden.

But still, what about the things she had told him? Like the wild way he made her feel? She shouldn't have said that, even if it was true. Everything about him sent her into a tailspin. When he'd sat next to her to help with the chopsticks, she'd barely been able to breathe. And now they were trapped in another of those strangely silent moments.

Their desserts finally arrived, giving them both something to do.

He picked up his spoon and broke into the crispy shell that surrounded the ice cream. "Have you ever made this?"

"No, but I always wanted to experiment with different recipes. In Asian cuisine, it's common to fry the ice cream in a tempura batter. But it can be made with cornflakes, nuts and cookie crumbles, too." She tasted the dollop on her spoon and let it melt in her mouth. Hers was covered in caramel sauce. He'd gotten his doused in chocolate.

"Dessert is always my favorite part of a meal. I snacked on all of the leftover pastries you sent home with me. I had to hit the gym a little harder this week, though."

She imagined him glistening with hard-earned sweat. "Why do the things that are so bad for us have to be so good?"

"That does seem to be the case. But indulging in the forbidden can be fun."

Or dangerous, she thought. If she indulged with him, heaven only knew what might happen. She still hadn't decided if she should let him kiss her tonight.

"Do you want to trade?" he asked.

"I'm sorry. What?"

"You can taste my ice cream, and I'll taste yours."

It was a common suggestion, she thought. People routinely shared desserts, but with him it struck her as sensual.

He slid his bowl toward her. "Here you go. Have some."

She followed his lead and nudged her bowl in his direction. She wished that he wasn't Kirby Talbot's son. If he was just a regular guy, she could let herself enjoy his company without guilt or fear.

They dipped into each other's ice cream at the same time. They even swallowed in unison.

"What do you think of mine?" he asked.

"It's just as good as mine." Sweet and crunchy and filled with flavor.

"Do you want to switch back or have another bite?"

"I'll take one more." Mary sucked down another spoonful of his ice cream and nearly moaned from the pleasure. The way he was watching her was making her feel sexual again.

After they returned to their own bowls, he asked, "Did you study art? Is it a requirement for becoming a pastry chef?"

She tried to act normal, to respond as if her body hadn't been betraying her. "No, it's not required. But pastry chefs need to be naturally creative and make their work look as appealing as it tastes." She added, "I took a few drawing classes in high school. I was always pretty good at it."

"I can't draw or paint worth a damn. But I'm a collector. I love going to museums and galleries and acquiring new pieces."

"I appreciate how art makes me feel. The emotion it can evoke. I hardly ever go to galleries or museums, though." That just wasn't part of her world.

"Maybe you can go with me."

Was he asking her out again already? He was definitely the most aggressive man she'd ever dated, but her experiences were limited. "So you can teach me how to be a connoisseur?"

"Sure, why not? My favorite is contemporary. But I collect modern, too."

"I always thought they were the same thing." Which proved how little she knew. "My high school art classes didn't cover that."

"Modern begins in the ninetieth century and ends around the 1970s. Contemporary is anything after that period and up to now, where it's forever changing." He leaned into the table. "I have collections in both of my houses."

"Both?"

"I have a city loft and an estate in the country. I don't spend as much time there. Sometimes I'm not even sure why I bought it, other than its proximity to Kirbyville."

The luxurious compound where he'd been raised, she thought, where his father still resided. She'd seen pictures of Kirbyville in the book. Mama hadn't been there, as Kirby had never brought her to his home. Their affair had taken place at a hotel, where Mama had been hidden away from Kirby's private life. But Brandon wasn't trying to keep Mary hidden. He'd already invited her to meet his family. For now, she just couldn't fathom it.

Continuing their conversation, she asked, "Why don't you spend more time at your country estate? And what was wrong with you buying it?"

"I just feel weird, sometimes, rattling around there alone. I have caretakers who run things, but it just seems like a waste of space for one person. I keep telling myself that I should offer it up for charity events, but I never do."

Mary used to help out at a soup kitchen back home, but that wasn't the same as what he was talking about. She wouldn't know his types of charities if they jumped out of a dozen cupcakes and bit her on the nose. "You could sell it."

"True. But then I'd have to relocate all of the art I have stored there."

"You do like your art."

"Yeah, I do. I even bought some paintings that you inspired."

She angled her head. "Do they have pastries in them? Are they hanging in your kitchen?"

He sat back in his seat. He'd already finished his ice cream. "They're in my bedroom at my loft."

Mary nearly fumbled with her spoon. It didn't take a genius to figure out that she'd motivated him to buy something sexy. She could see it in his eyes, hear it in his voice. His bedroom was an obvious giveaway, too. She tried for a joke. "And here I thought they were depictions of éclairs or cream puffs."

He smiled a little. "No, I can't say that they are."

"Silly me." She tried to shrug off her discomfort. "But I think it's time to wrap things up. I have to be at the bakery at 4:00 a.m. tomorrow."

"Do you always work that early?"

"Yes. But I'm basically a morning person, so it's okay." She prattled on, attempting to get the paintings off her mind. "Plus I have weekends off. At least it's a fairly normal schedule."

"I'm a morning person, too. That's why I roll out of bed on Sundays and take Cline for those bright-eyed-and-bushy-tailed walks." He motioned to their waiter, letting him know they were ready for their bill. "But I'll let you go so you can get some sleep."

He paused, his gaze riveted to hers. "Of course, I'm going to have to insist on escorting you to your car. I don't want to lose you that easily."

Because he was still hoping to kiss her, she thought. As passionately as he could.

Four

Mary and Brandon stood beside her car, an old Toyota that she'd scrimped and saved to buy. Brandon's fancy new BMW was parked a few spaces away. If she hadn't been feeling the class difference between them before, she was certainly feeling it now. Of course, it was crazy to say that she hadn't been feeling it before. Wealth and power illuminated him like the sun. Or *the son*, she thought, of one of Nashville's most successful superstars. Thank God he didn't look like Kirby. If he favored his father, she didn't think she could tolerate being this close to him. She certainly wouldn't want him the way she did. A want. A need. A disaster waiting to happen.

She backed herself against the driver's door of her car. But that was a bad move. That only allowed him to step even closer, pinning her in place and using his body as the anchor.

He looked sharp and fashionable in clothes, but she suspected that he would look even better naked.

Really? She was thinking about that now? Yes, damn it, she was. And she suspected that if she pulled his shirt out from where it was tucked into his pants and tore the buttons open, she would find rock-hard abs underneath.

She hadn't seen any shirtless pictures of him. He didn't post that kind. No beachfront vacation shots, nothing that bared him to the public. But she was filling in the blanks.

He said, "When I was a teenager, I used to take my dates to this pretty spot in the country to make out." He reached out to skim his knuckles across her cheek. "I've never made out in a parking lot with streetlights glaring overhead."

His touch, just that one simple touch, made her shiver. "We aren't making out. We're just standing here."

"We aren't teenagers, either." He ran his thumb across her mouth, even rolling it across the inside of her bottom lip and making his thumb wet.

Foreplay to a kiss, she thought. If she hadn't been braced against the car, she might've lost her footing.

"Are you going to let me kiss you?" he asked. "Are you going to let this happen?"

She should've told him, "No." But she whispered a soft and throaty, "Yes."

He did it. He captured her lips, dragging her under his spell and stealing the last of her sanity.

His tongue made contact with hers, and she moaned into his mouth. He cupped her chin, and she made another pleasured sound. Lust burned her skin, scorching her, heating her from the inside out. She wrapped her arms around him, pulling him tighter, wanting to scorch him, too.

Was he as aroused as she was? Was he hard and hungry, his muscles bunching, his body tingling?

They rubbed and kissed, two people who barely knew each other, going PDA outside a popular restaurant.

He came to his senses first and eased away from her. Now that it was over, ambient sounds merged into focus and abraded her ears. Other patrons were walking to their cars and talking.

"Mary, Mary, quite contrary…" Brandon's voice was rough. "I don't think I ever thought about that rhyme until now."

Her mother used to recite it to her, but hearing him say it was a whole other matter. "I don't think I'm going to be able to sleep tonight."

"That's not good. I'm already keeping you from your bed."

Her bed was going to be a dicey place from now on. "My room gets hot sometimes. The air-conditioning vent in there never seems to work right, and the maintenance department at our building isn't so great about fixing things."

"So that's what's going to keep you up? A humid summer night in Tennessee?"

He was making the weather seem more humid than it was. But the world seemed hotter and stickier with Brandon Talbot in it. "Summers in Oklahoma can be this way, too."

"What do you sleep in to stay cool?" he asked, making her throat go dry.

This was beginning to sound like phone sex, but they were talking eye to eye, face-to-face. "Just whatever feels right." Her panties and bra, an old T-shirt, a lightweight nightgown. But tonight, she was tempted to sleep naked, to thrash and moan and fantasize about him. "I better go now."

"All right, but when are we going see each other again?"

In her dreams, she thought. Or maybe it would be in her nightmares. She was getting hooked on a man who'd helped hurt her mother. Even if he hadn't done it purposely, he was still connected to Mama's pain.

"When, Mary?" he asked again.

"I don't know." Her confusion was growing by leaps and bounds. "Let's figure it out later."

"Okay." He leaned in to kiss her again. But this time, it was gentlemanly, a protective peck on the cheek. "Will you text me to let me know you got home safe?"

She nodded, then turned to open her car door. She climbed behind the wheel and locked herself inside, afraid that she would never feel safe again.

* * *

The following week, Mary spent Saturday afternoon with Brandon. She'd had nine days to recover from his kiss. But she wasn't doing a very good job of bouncing back. He was all she thought about.

Once again, she took her own car and met him at the designated location: a gallery that specialized in naïve art. Mary didn't even know that genre existed, but she soon learned that it referred to works created by artists who lacked formal training. Most of it seemed to have a childlike perspective, concentrating on animals, people and plants, rather than inanimate objects. She noticed lots of bold colors, too.

As they wandered the brightly lit gallery, Brandon said, "I'm looking for a piece to give Tommy and Sophie for the nursery. The due date is getting closer, and I want to send something over before the baby arrives." He stopped in front of a painting that depicted trees that resembled lollipops. "They're having a girl, and they're going to name her Zoe. They're using Sloane as her middle name because that was Sophie's mom's name, and they want to honor her. Sophie's mom died soon after Sophie was born. Her dad is gone, too. He passed away a few years back."

"Oh, I'm so sorry for her losses." Mary gazed at the lollipop-tree picture, which also had a rainbow shooting across the sky and a river with fish jumping out of the water. "I understand how she feels. But it's just so hard to…" She let her words drift. She could feel him watching her.

A second later, he said, "I understand that talking

about your parents is difficult. But if you ever need anyone to confide in, I'm a good listener."

"Thank you." He was the last person she could confide in about her parents. Needing to redirect his attention, she gestured to the painting. "Are you considering this one for Zoe's nursery?"

He shook his head. "I don't think it's girlie enough. They decorated in pink, with bows and frills and whatnot. So I'd like to find something along that vein."

"Do they have a theme? Like butterflies or flowers or anything?"

"They put silver stars on the ceiling. I think that has something to do with how they'd stargazed in Texas when they were visiting Matt and Libby. But it's not a theme, per se. Mostly the room is just pink and pretty." He paused and added, "I don't have any experience with babies, but I'm excited about being an uncle. It's been fun getting to know Libby's son, too. Chance is a charming kid."

Mary nodded. Seven-year-old Chance had been mentioned in the book, in particular that he'd been named after one of Kirby's most famous songs. Libby was widowed, and she and her late husband were fans of Kirby's long before she'd ever been hired to be his biographer.

Brandon continued by saying, "There's a lot going on with my brothers this summer. Not just with Tommy and Sophie's daughter coming into the world, but also with Matt and Libby. Their wedding is in August."

There was nothing going on with her or Alice, aside from them trying to give Mama the vindication she deserved. Mary envied Brandon the happy journeys his family was embarking upon.

"Thanks for coming here with me," he said. "It's going to help to have a woman's touch in picking something out."

"You could have hired someone to choose something. Or told the gallery what you were looking for." He had all sorts of people at his disposal. Even the gallery owner knew him by name. "You don't really need me."

"I think I do." He reached for her hand.

She threaded her fingers through his, tighter than she should have. The more time she spent with him, the more her attraction to him escalated. She already felt as if she was being seduced by him, maybe even in the same way his father had seduced her mother.

How long would it be before she tumbled into bed with him? Before he did wicked things to her? Mary suspected that Mama had resisted Kirby at first, too.

But she kept telling herself that she wasn't going to sleep with Brandon. That she didn't want to carry her revenge that far.

Needing a diversion, she let go of his hand and walked over to a picture called *Magic*.

Brandon followed her and looked at it, too. Then he said, "That's too grown-up for a baby's room."

"I know. I was just admiring it." A crimson-haired fairy was blowing dandelions into the wind. She definitely had an adult quality, as if she might be a siren of sorts. Naïve art could obviously showcase mature subjects, too. "I think it's alluring."

"I can buy it for you."

She started. "What?"

"I said that I can buy that painting for you. Do you want it, Mary? Do you want to take it home and put it in your bedroom?"

"You don't have to buy me anything." She wasn't comfortable accepting gifts from him.

"But it's obvious how drawn you are to it. And the fairy is a redhead, like you."

"That isn't why she appeals to me." Then again, maybe it was. But she didn't want to say that.

He moved closer, nuzzling his cheek against her hair. "It would be nice to know that she's watching over you at night, creating enchantment while you sleep."

He was intensifying the moment, making the fairy an instrument of desire between them. "Will you tell me about the paintings you have in your room?" she asked, curious to know what pictures she'd inspired.

He all but whispered his response. "They're erotic, but they're romantic, too. Nothing like I've ever bought before."

She spoke just as softly, not wanting anyone to overhear them. "It's strange, knowing you got them because of me."

"I couldn't seem to help it."

And she couldn't help feeling aroused by the idea. But nonetheless, she shouldn't be having this conversation with him. They'd come here to find something for Zoe's nursery, not talk about erotic art.

They continued to browse. A short time later, Mary came across a painting with a pink-and-purple carousel, an animated piece with joyous energy.

"This is adorable," she said. "It even has ribbons and bows on the frame."

"That is pretty cool." Brandon smiled like the expectant uncle he was. "Totally perfect for a nursery. I knew you'd be my good luck charm today."

She stayed in the background while he purchased the painting, and after he made the transaction, he said, "They're going to ship it to Tommy's house." They walked outside and he added, "I wish you would've let me buy the fairy for you."

"Buying me gifts isn't necessary." She wasn't comfortable being put in that position. None of this was comfortable.

"Okay, but this is getting crazy, with you taking your own car every time we go out. You have to start trusting me, Mary."

The way her mother had trusted his father? The comparison set her on edge. "It's only our second date."

"And we need to make the most of it. Let's go to my loft. We can fix some lunch and eat on the roof." He moved closer. "Cline would love to see you."

She inhaled the enticing scent of his skin. "Are you using your dog as bait to get me to go home with you?"

"Yes, I am." He took her into his arms and hugged her, warm and tight, using that as bait, too.

Brandon had never chased anyone the way he was chasing Mary. He'd never had to. The women he dated fit naturally into the world he'd carved out for himself, but Mary seemed reluctant to be part of it. So he'd wanted to buy her a gift? So what? His other lovers would have accepted it without hesitation. Of course, Mary wasn't his lover. But that shouldn't matter. It was just a painting.

He looked in his rearview mirror. She was following him in her car. At least he'd gotten her to come to his loft. He was eager to spend the rest of the afternoon with her.

She was an enigma and so was her family. A wild sister and deceased parents she didn't want to talk about. Brandon wasn't a morbidly curious person. But he did wonder how she'd lost her parents. Was it an accident? Had they died recently? Or had they been gone a long time?

Maybe once he met her sister, he would get a better feel for who Mary was. Except that she hadn't offered to introduce him to Alice. Was she keeping him away from her apartment because she wasn't ready for him to get acquainted with Alice? Or was he reading more into this than there was?

He'd already taken the liberty of checking out Alice's Instagram, and she was just as Mary had described her: a party girl with a flair for fashion. As far as he could tell, Mary didn't do any social media. But he intended to ask her about it.

At least he knew that Mary was close to her sister, with how often she talked about her. Brandon had always been tight with his family. Once he decided to become an attorney, he'd specialized in entertainment law so he could represent his parents and Tommy. He had other clients, but his family was his priority.

Even when he'd first heard about his half brother, when he'd learned his dad had a secret kid out there, Brandon was interested in Matt. Blood was blood, as far as he was concerned.

He rechecked his mirror, making sure Mary was still behind him. He couldn't begin to guess what kind of childhood she'd had, but he suspected that she'd had a hand in raising her sister. Or she was at least trying to provide some sort of guidance now.

He turned onto a side street and entered a small underground parking structure, using a code to open the gate. Once he parked, he motioned to Mary, telling her to take the space next to him.

They exited their vehicles, and she asked, "Where is everyone else? All of the other cars?"

"Everyone else parks on the other side, from a different entrance. This is my private lot." He guided her toward an elevator. "That's mine, too. It requires a key to open it."

"You have your own parking lot and your own elevator?"

"I own the building. I lease space to other tenants, but I like having this part of it to myself. The entire top floor and the roof are mine, too. Over-all, it's a great location, and it's close to my office." He unlocked the elevator. "Sometimes convenience matters." To make life easier, he thought. But at the moment, it didn't seem easy.

They stepped inside, and he pushed the button. She stood near the wall and smoothed the front of her loose-fitting blouse.

Brandon ran his gaze over her, aroused by her modesty. He'd never made love in an elevator, and he was fairly certain that she'd never done it, either. Funny thing, too. His friends kept telling him that he should start seeing nice girls. But nice girls weren't supposed to trigger these types of fantasies.

The ride was painfully quiet. He was still fixated on elevator sex.

Once the door opened onto his floor, he led her down the hall. With how the loft was designed, his front door was at the very end, and now it seemed like a long and grueling walk. "In the future, I can give you the code to the gate and a key to the eleva-tor so you can come up here on your own."

She furrowed her brow. "How many codes and keys have you given out?"

"Honestly? None."

"Then how do people visit you?"

"I leave their names at the security desk, and the guard in the lobby notifies me when they arrive. For my regular visitors, their names are always on the list. But Security still lets me know when they're here."

She stopped walking, the sconce lighting in the hallway illuminating her face. "But you'd let me bypass your security?"

"Yes." With how strong his fantasies were about her, he was willing to make an exception. "I can give you a key to the loft itself, and then you can just come over whenever you want to see me." To offer herself to him, he thought. To become his lover. "Maybe even in the middle of the night when I least expect you."

She fussed with the front of her blouse again, plucking at imaginary lint. She seemed to need to keep her hands busy. "I can't imagine doing that."

"Maybe in time you will." He could tell she was as attracted to him as he was to her. But he didn't know if she would follow through. That remained to be seen. "For today, we're just having lunch." He paused. "And maybe a kiss, too."

She glanced up at him. "Are you sure we should...?"

"Yeah, I'm sure." He leaned in and slanted his mouth over hers.

She reacted with immediate passion, and he appreciated how quick she was to enjoy it. As their tongues sparred, she made sexy little sounds. He cupped her rear, pulling her closer. The security camera in the hallway was probably capturing their every move. But he didn't care. He might even watch the tape later. He had access to it from his computer.

Damn, he thought. He could have eaten her alive.

But as exciting as it was, he ended it before he got carried away. The only hunger they were going to sate this afternoon would be for food.

Although Mary was still reeling from Brandon's kiss, she was captivated by his loft, too. His home was beautiful, with banks of floor-to-ceiling windows. He'd decorated with black and gray furniture, creating a strong and masculine vibe. His art collection was magnificent. But for whatever reason, he left his bedroom off the tour, along with the artwork she'd inspired. Maybe before this visit was over, she would ask him to show her those paintings. But for now, she couldn't find the strength to do it, not after he'd invited her to come to him in the middle of the night. She needed time to wrap her head around that.

She walked over to one of the windows in the living room, and Cline followed her. She'd already seen the dog's room earlier. He had his own luxurious space that included a king-size bed and a TV that was programmed to an animal channel.

"This is a spectacular view," she said to Brandon. "I'll bet it's really pretty at night, twinkling with city lights."

He joined her and the dog at the window. "You can come by any night and find out."

She chastised him. "You need to stop saying things like that to me."

"Sorry. It's just the effect you have on me. I'm not usually this badly behaved." He motioned to the husky. "Cline looks like he's trying to protect you from me."

"Maybe he is." The dog kept moving closer to her.

"Cline has definitely taken a shine to you. I think he might even like you better than he likes Rob." He checked her out. "But you're prettier than Rob."

She struggled to ignore Brandon's flirtation. "I have no idea who you're talking about."

"Rob is my dog sitter. He watches Cline when I go out of town. He walks him while I'm at work, too. Sometimes Cline goes on play dates with Rob's Lab."

"Oh, that's nice." She was glad that Cline had a friend. She patted the pooch's head. Then she asked Brandon, "Do you have a housekeeper who does scheduled cleanings?" She already knew that he didn't have a live-in. His guest rooms were unoccupied. But his loft was also spotless.

"Yes, I do," he responded casually. "Her name is Pearl."

She contemplated his life and the people in it. "And how do Pearl and Rob enter your loft?"

"They each have a key to the front door." He softened his voice. "But it's not the same as me giving you one."

She fought a sexy shiver. "Because they still check in with the guard when they arrive?"

"Yes, but also because they were screened before I hired them. As high-profile as my family is, I have to be careful who I let in here."

"That's understandable." She forced a smile, made

a joke. "I guess I'm lucky you let me in. But your interest in me is something altogether different."

"That's for sure." He hesitated before he said, "I hope this doesn't sound creepy, but I looked up your sister's Instagram. I was curious about her."

"It's fine." She'd actually expected him to do that at some point. But she also knew there wasn't anything in it that she hadn't already divulged about Alice. "Everyone looks each other up these days."

"Why don't you do social media? I wanted to follow you on some of the sites I use, but I couldn't find you. You're not using another name, are you?"

"No." She downplayed her reasoning. "I deleted my accounts when Alice and I moved to Nashville. I did it when I convinced her to shut hers down. Only she started up again, and I didn't. I was never very active anyway. It just isn't my thing." Thankfully, that was true. She wasn't a social media hound.

"I do a lot of it. Not as much as Tommy and my dad, but I'm still out there."

"I know. I looked at your pages. You weren't the only one poking around online." She figured it sounded like the normal behavior now that they were dating. She couldn't admit that she'd done it before they'd met. "You have lots of pictures of Cline. He's your online star."

"He definitely is. But he's really into you right now."

She nodded. The dog was still standing protectively beside her. "Has he ever done this with any of your other female guests?"

"No. He appreciates Pearl, though. But she washes his bedding and fluffs his pillows. Just for the record, Pearl isn't just my housekeeper. She's also married to my chef. He makes meals for me and leaves them in the fridge."

"Are they an older couple?" She was curious about the husband-and-wife team.

"They're in their midfifties. They're great together, like one entity. But that's how it should be with people who are meant for each other, I guess. Tommy and Sophie seem like that now, too. My parents never made sense. They're better as friends than they were as spouses."

She wished that she could tell him more about her parents, how they were never married and how much she missed her mom. But he was the last man in the world she could tell her secrets to. She was already getting closer to him than she could bear.

"Do you like me, Mary?"

She nearly flinched. "Why are you asking me that?" Had he just read her mind?

"I can tell that you're attracted to me. But that's not the same as liking me."

She shifted her gaze back to the cityscape. She was too antsy to keep looking at him. "Yes, I like you. Maybe even a bit too much."

"There's no such thing as liking someone too much. And just so you know, I like you, too." He took her hand and held it. "Come to the kitchen, and we'll make lunch."

"What are we making?"

"I figured we could throw some sandwiches together. I have some leftover potato salad Chef made. I always have fresh fruit on hand, too. There's a nice big bowl of strawberries already cleaned and sliced."

"I could go for that." She attempted to relax, to not think too deeply about how much she liked him. He was wrong that you couldn't care for someone too much. In her case, she shouldn't be getting attached to him at all.

They worked naturally together in the kitchen, moving like well-oiled machines. The sandwiches they'd decided to "throw together" were grilled cheese.

"You're a pretty good cook," she said.

"This is barely cooking." He flipped the sandwiches on the grill of his professional-quality stove. "I could never make the stuff Chef makes for me." He glanced over at her. "But I sure as hell like watching you."

Mary's heart skipped a beat. She was making fresh whipping cream for the strawberries. "This is right up my alley."

"You should have seen me with the treats you baked for me. I kept them in my room and ate them when I was in bed, like a kid, getting crumbs all over the covers."

There was nothing kid-like about Brandon, she thought. But his description of himself made her laugh, anyway.

He came over to her. "I like it when you do that."

"Do what?"

"Laugh."

"It struck me as funny." She attempted to shoo him away. "But now you need to go back to your side of the kitchen."

"Not until I have a little taste—" he stuck a spoon into the whipping cream "—of this."

She rolled her eyes. "Now you're just being a pest."

"I know." He had a sinful expression on his face as he swallowed the cream, looking hotter than a man had a right to be.

When he put down the spoon, she wondered if he was going to kiss her, the way he'd done in the hallway.

But he returned to the sandwiches, leaving her suddenly longing for more.

Five

The roof had been designed for entertaining, with a built-in barbecue, a fire pit, a bar, whatever Brandon needed. There was a fenced area for Cline, too. Mary was impressed, but everything about Brandon's life was impressive. She couldn't imagine being so successful. But Mama used to dream about it. If it hadn't mattered so much to her, she wouldn't have gone to Nashville, hoping to sell her songs.

Mary studied Brandon in the sunlight. They sat at a patio table that was anchored to the rooftop. He'd already eaten his sandwich and was working his way through the potato salad, eager, it seemed, to get to the strawberries. She was alternating bites, eating bits of everything at once.

"How much time do you spend up here?" she asked.

He lifted his head. "As much time as I can."

"It certainly is private."

"I grew up in a fishbowl, so I like my privacy at home. Tommy and my dad have bodyguards. But I don't need that kind of security. It's one of the perks of *not* being famous."

He wasn't a celebrity. But he seemed like one to her, with his chiseled features and natural sophistication. Someone could easily play him in a movie.

"How do you screen your employees?" she asked.

She assumed he did more than just check out their social media presence. Of course, a lot could be uncovered online, which was why she and Alice had been so careful.

He replied, "I use a service for security screenings. My biggest nightmare would be hiring someone who's only interested in working for me so they can get close to my family."

She defended the masses. "Everyone out there isn't a crazed fan, Brandon."

"I didn't say they were. Dad and Tommy have some amazing fans, people who love and respect them. But some of their admirers have gone too far. They've both had their fair share of stalkers."

Mary's heart froze in her chest. She shouldn't have steered their conversation in this direction, not at the risk of him getting suspicious of her. He'd already been cautious, on the day they'd first met.

"I'm sorry," he said. "I'm making everything sound so dangerous. Really, it's not that bad."

No, she thought. It was worse. Her mother was one of the "supposed" stalkers he was talking about.

"Should we change the subject?" he asked.

"Yes, please." She couldn't stand another second of it.

"All right. How about this? Tell me something about yourself, something that you haven't told me before."

"I don't know what to say." She was still feeling like the worst kind of liar, keeping her identity from him.

"Just say whatever pops into your head."

She searched the recesses of her mind for something honest and true. "I used to sing in the church choir. I'm not very good. But it was something both Alice and I did." Their mother had encouraged it. Music had meant everything to Mama. She was an accomplished singer and an even better songwriter.

"Well, you've got me beat. I don't sing or play an instrument or do any of that. I never showed an aptitude for it." He sipped a bottled iced tea. "I grew up around creative people, but I went the corporate route instead."

"You're an entertainment lawyer who collects art. I'd say that you fit in with creative people just fine."

"Yeah, I guess I do." He leaned farther forward in his chair. "Why haven't you asked to see the paintings in my room?"

Her nerves jumped to attention. She turned the

question around on him. "Why didn't you offer to show me?"

"Because I was waiting for you to ask. Or hoping you would, anyway."

"I was building up the courage." She noticed that he was going after his strawberries and cream now. "Will you show me when we're done eating?"

He nodded and smiled. "I'd be glad to."

She glanced down at her plate. Was she asking for trouble by going into his bedroom? By seeing where he slept? By getting a firsthand view of the paintings he'd bought because of her? Yes, she thought, she was. But she was going to do it, anyway.

After lunch, they returned to the loft. As soon as they entered his bedroom, Mary got warm all over, heat shooting through her veins. The paintings, three of them, were above his bed.

She moved closer, curious to see every detail. They were abstract nudes, done in oil, big and bold and bursting with color.

Each of them depicted a man and woman together, in various positions of foreplay. Their faces were obscured. In that sense, they could have been anyone. The woman had long straight hair, falling past her shoulders, mostly in shades of red and highlighted with blue and purple. She was lean and fluid, and her lover was rife with strength and power.

Mary couldn't stop staring at them. In the third painting the man was on his knees, preparing to make the woman come.

"So now you know what you inspired," Brandon said.

She turned to meet his gaze. "They're beautiful. But they scare me, too." Her heart pounded at every pulse point of her body. "To know that's how you think of me."

"I've done a lot of things in my life and been with a lot of women, but no one has ever made me feel this way."

She admitted how he affected her. "From the day I met you, I was worried that if I slept with you, you would dominate me. That you'd be dangerous to my soul."

"Maybe I am. But maybe you're dangerous to me, too."

She definitely was, she thought. "But us being together is wrong. We don't belong in each other's worlds." There was too much at stake, too much history he didn't know about.

"When we were in the elevator, I was fantasizing about making love to you there. All these years I've had a private elevator and I've never ravished anyone in it."

Just the fact that he'd used the word *ravished* made her imagination run wild. "Sex is all it could ever be. And then it would have to end. It would have to be over."

He frowned. "You're talking about ending it before it's even begun."

She walked over to a metal armoire on the other side of the room, trying to put distance between them. "I shouldn't be talking about it happening at all. I can't sleep with you. I can't do this."

His breath rushed out. "I'm not asking you to be with me right this second."

"I can't keep dating you." Everything about it was a mistake.

"Don't cut and run, Mary. Give it a chance."

"But I'm so confused." She wanted to come to his loft in the middle of night and make love with him. But she wanted to disappear, too, and never see him again. At this point, she was even more conflicted over taking her revenge out on him. It just didn't feel right anymore. But maybe it never really did. Either way, she'd gotten herself tangled up in an emotional mess. "I don't know what to do."

He opened a nightstand drawer. "My extra keys are in here, to the elevator and to the loft." He approached her and dropped them into her hand. "In case you decide to use them."

She didn't reply. She couldn't think beyond the lust. She could still see the paintings from where she stood.

He said, "The code to the gate is Mona Lisa, spelled out in numbers." When she blinked at him, he shrugged. "I'm fascinated by her smile." He roughly added, "I like yours, too."

She wasn't smiling now. She was clutching the keys so tightly in her palm that she feared the edges would cut her. "I have to go."

"I hope you come back. I really hope you do."

Mary couldn't make any promises. She darted out

of his room and grabbed her purse from the living room where she'd left it.

He followed her to the front door, and she said goodbye and turned to leave. But whether she was coming back again, she couldn't say. For now, she just needed to escape.

A week had passed since Brandon saw Mary, since she'd disappeared from his loft. He waited for her every night, hoping to see her, but she never showed up.

He hadn't called or texted. He didn't want to pressure her. But he ached every minute of the day. He had it bad. He'd never wanted anyone so much. He was drowning in his own desire.

"What the hell is wrong with you?" his dad asked.

Brandon glanced up. His father was in a mood. But so was he. "Nothing is wrong." He wasn't going to admit that he had a woman on his mind.

He and Dad were seated in the main parlor at Kirbyville. As always, Dad was dressed in black, with his graying beard neatly trimmed. Brandon couldn't remember a time when Kirby looked like anything except an outlaw. But that was his persona. Tommy's, too, for that matter, even if Tommy had a more youthful sense of style.

Dad scowled. "I asked you to come by because I have something to discuss with you, and you look like you're spacing out."

"I'm just sipping my brandy." Brandon swirled the amber liquid in his snifter. His recovering-alcoholic father was sipping ginger ale. "So what's going on? What do you want to talk about?"

"Your mother, for one."

Brandon cocked his head. During the divorce, his parents had fought like rabid cats and flea-bitten dogs, but that was when Brandon and Tommy were teenagers. A lot of time had passed since then. Both his mom and dad were thrilled about becoming grandparents. They couldn't wait for Zoe to be born.

Dad moved to the edge of his seat. "Your mom has a new boyfriend. Some dude who works in finance."

Brandon wasn't alarmed. His mother dated now and then. But it was never anything serious. After what she'd been through with Kirby, she was careful not to get too wrapped up in anyone. "Is that a problem for you?"

"No. But I was thinking that maybe it's time for me to start dating, too."

"Does that mesh with your sobriety? Have you talked to your counselor about this?"

"Yes, and he said as long as it's healthy dating, it'll be all right."

"That makes sense." Except the crazy thing was, Brandon wasn't even sure if healthy dating factored into how he was feeling, not with how hungry he was for Mary.

Dad guzzled his ginger ale. "I'm a little nervous about getting back out there."

Brandon was nervous, too, but for a different reason. He was worried that he might never see Mary again. "Maybe you should give it more time. You've got a lot going on, with becoming a grandparent."

"I can still be a grandpa and have a girlfriend. It gets lonely not having anyone to share my life with."

"Have you discussed this with Tommy?"

"Yes, and he wasn't as supportive as I'd hoped he'd be." Dad got up and moved about the parlor. "He isn't convinced that I've changed, not where women are concerned, anyway."

"I think you have." Or it certainly seemed that way, particularly with how much this appeared to matter to him. "But it's still a big step, and you still need to be sure you're ready."

Dad sighed. "Does that mean I have your blessing?"

"You don't need my blessing to go out there and date. That's something you need to tackle on your own. But I'll be around anytime you need to a shoulder to lean on."

"Thank you for understanding. I wish Tommy was more like you. Matt could take a few pointers from you, too."

If Brandon wasn't so mixed-up about Mary, he might've laughed. "I'm just not as hotheaded as my brothers." Yet at the moment, their lives were far more centered than his.

Kirby grinned. "You've always been my favorite."

Brandon shook his head. "You shouldn't say things like that, Pop."

"I was just kidding." His dad chuckled. An instant later, he turned serious and said, "I love all my boys. You're all special to me. But I always feel better when I bring my problems to you."

"Glad I could help." Brandon wasn't going to bring his problems to anyone. He was just going to wait to see what happened with Mary.

Mary sat in her room, surfing the net on her phone for something to do. It was ten fifteen, and on a Friday night, no less. Most people her age would be out on the town. Or curled up with a significant other or doing something besides fretting alone in bed. She couldn't stop thinking about Brandon, and watching stupid YouTube videos wasn't helping.

She got up and went into the kitchen to get a glass of sweet tea from the pitcher she and Alice kept in the fridge. Her sister wasn't home. She'd gone out with friends. Already Alice had a peer group in Nashville. A bunch of wildings, no doubt, that she'd met on a social app, but at least she was off having a good time.

Mary liked her new coworkers, but she didn't have enough in common with them to hang out outside the job.

She missed her friends in Oklahoma City. She hadn't told any of them the truth of why she'd come to Nashville, though. None of them even knew about her mom's affair with Kirby Talbot or that he'd filed a restraining order against her. Mama was too ashamed to admit that Kirby had duped her, so she'd done her darnedest to keep it a secret, and so had Mary and Alice.

And now, of course, there was Brandon, and Mary's dilemma with him. Should she go to his loft tonight, return his keys and tell him that it was over for good? No more dates? No more kisses? No more talk of sex?

If she ended it now, everyone could go on with their lives without Brandon ever knowing the truth. The initial plan was to get Brandon hooked on her, then dump him in a cold and calculating way, revealing her deception to him and his father. But if Mary stopped seeing Brandon without telling him or Kirby who she was, then at least she wouldn't be deliberating hurting him or rubbing his face in it. She just wanted the revenge to go away. Alice wouldn't like it, but it wasn't up to her. Mary had the right to break free, to stop seeing Brandon, to stop dating him and playing this terrible game.

Yes, she thought. She was going to end this madness once and for all. But she wasn't going to show up unannounced. This wasn't a booty call. She wasn't going to use the keys he'd given her and slip into his bedroom. No matter how thrilling sleeping with him sounded, Mary wasn't a fool. She knew an affair with him would result in disaster.

She finished her tea and returned to her room for her phone. He might not even be home. If that was the case, then she would just have to wait to hear back from him.

For now, she sent a text. Are you at the loft? Is it okay if I stop by? Need to talk.

He responded immediately with Now? Tonight?

Her heart flew to her throat. Yes, she texted back. But just to talk. She wanted to make sure he'd gotten that part.

Sure. Come over. I'm here.

She had no idea how he was feeling. You could never tell with texts unless someone used emoticons, and even then sometimes people posted smiley faces when they weren't smiling for real.

Winding down the conversation, she typed, I'll see you in a while. Need to get ready.

Okay. See you, too.

She tossed her phone back on the bed and headed for the shower.

Once she was standing beneath the spray of water, naked as the day she was born, she closed her eyes.

And tried not to think about Brandon.

But he swirled through her mind like a mist. She opened her eyes and pumped a glob of bath gel into her hands. Still thinking about him, she lathered her body.

If she touched herself, would the ache go away?

No, she thought. Pressing her fingers between her legs wasn't going to help her cause. She needed to do this cold turkey. Determined to stay strong, she finished her shower, taking extra care in washing and conditioning her hair.

After she toweled off, she blow-dried her hair and styled it in its usual French braid. She slipped on a plain white bra and matching panties. Not that her underwear mattered. She was the only one who was going to see them. But she was trying to keep her appearance as low-key as possible, even for herself. She chose a simple cotton dress with sunflowers on it, a pair of yellow sneakers and a pale pink cardigan that matched her lip gloss. She barely had any eye makeup on. The less sexy she looked, the less likely she was to feel sexy.

Or so she hoped.

A short time later, when she arrived at the big iron gate at Brandon's building, she fumbled with the code. She had to keep looking at the dial pad on her phone to punch in the corresponding numbers for Mona Lisa. She should have written them down before she got here.

Finally, the gate opened, admitting her into Brandon's private parking area. Although it was well lit, it still seemed eerie and isolated.

She made a beeline for the elevator and used the key. After she stepped inside, she wished that Brandon hadn't told her about his elevator sex fantasy. She bit down on her bottom lip to keep from getting turned on.

So much for not feeling sexy.

She cursed her lack of self-control, nearly running out of the elevator when the door rolled open.

Still struggling with her composure, she walked down the hallway to Brandon's front door. She knocked, the way any proper guest should do.

He answered her summons with his eyes seeming darker than usual, like a midnight sky instead of their typical daytime blue. She entered his home, and they stared at each other.

He whispered her name, and she lost her resolve. Like a woman possessed, she moved closer and leaned into him.

Just one kiss, she thought, as their lips connected. One sweet, sensual kiss before she ended it for good.

Six

Mary didn't stop at one kiss. She pressed harder against Brandon, eager to devour him. He reacted just as eagerly, just as desperately. He backed her against the door, and she dropped her purse onto the floor with a resounding thud and used both arms to cling to him.

He tasted as thick and rich as her favorite devil's food cake, soaked in rum. She was already getting drunk on him. Slick, wet, openmouthed kisses. Could it get any hotter?

She wanted to make frenzied love with him, to have full-on, tear-each-other-apart, animalistic sex.

Right here. Right now.

Mindless, feverish…

Sex, sex, sex…

Was she crazy having those kinds of thoughts?

They came up for air, and she could barely see straight. Nothing was right in her head.

He dropped to his knees, and she fought the fuzziness in her brain. He looked damned fine, kneeling before her, making her heart spin. Trying to process her emotions, she said, "I came here to give your keys back, to never see you again."

"We can talk about that later." He reached under her dress and peeled her panties down her legs.

Mary thought about the artwork in his room. She knew exactly where Brandon's mouth was going to go. "Should I take my dress all the way off?"

"No." He skimmed his hands along her inner thighs. "You can just hold it up for me."

Oh, my. If she wasn't so aroused, she would have blushed. "Can I watch?"

"Absolutely. But you still have to lift your dress for me."

She gathered the hem and raised it an inch at a time. She'd never done anything so brazen before. But she wanted to feel his mouth on her.

"You look pretty tonight," he said. "Sweet and wholesome."

"I was just trying to look like my usual self." Plain, she thought. Simple. But there was nothing simple about the way Brandon was making her feel. She bunched her dress around her hips, exposing herself to him.

He parted her with his thumbs, and she tightened

her hold on the fabric in her hands. The bright yellow sunflowers…

He went for it, using his tongue in the most delicious of ways. Mary mewled like a kitten. Or maybe she was rumbling like a mountain lion.

She wanted to tug on Brandon's hair, but she couldn't. Being deprived of touching him made the ache between her legs more pronounced. She lifted her dress even higher.

"That's right," he said. "Show me more."

He increased the heat, the pleasure, the forbidden sensations. He was being relentless, making swirling motions with his tongue. He used his fingers, too. Mary watched him as if her life depended on his very existence. And maybe it did. Maybe she hadn't been alive, *really alive*, until tonight.

She climaxed, feeling hot and frenzied.

When she was done, she feared she might topple over. She was still clutching her dress around her hips.

He stood and smiled. "Now you can take it all the way off."

She removed her dress, along with her sweater, and he reached around to unhook her bra.

Once she was bare, he said, "We need to take this into the bedroom. That's where the protection is."

He scooped her up like a naked bride about to be carried over the threshold. Fascinated with the way he made her feel, she put her hand against his cheek. His skin was warm, his jaw cleanly shaved.

He shouldered his way into his room, where the paintings glimmered in the soft light.

He placed her on the bed and began tugging at his clothes. It was then that she realized he was wearing a novelty T-shirt that said Trust Me, I'm a Lawyer across the front of it.

Could he be trusted? God, she hoped so.

But for now, she just wanted to put her hands all over him.

Brandon sucked in his breath. Mary's touch felt sweet, but wicked, too. So damned good, he thought. She stroked him, making him harder than he already was.

He didn't want to think about the fact that she'd been prepared to return his keys and stop seeing him. All that mattered was that she'd changed her mind.

"I love how you came for me," he said. "How you looked at me when I was putting my mouth on you."

"I love how it felt." She ran her thumb across the tip of him, making a pearly bead of semen appear. "I knew that you'd dominate me if we ever slept together."

"Oh, yeah?" He rolled over on top of her, pressing his nakedness against hers. "How so?"

"Just that you'd overpower my senses." She writhed beneath him, creating sexy friction.

"Maybe I should dominate you in other ways, too." He grabbed her wrists and cuffed them with his hands, holding her arms above her head. "I've never been into handcuffs or blindfolds or anything like that, but with you anything seems possible." He wanted to explore the woman she was, to unfold her mystery, to draw her into the deepest, darkest recesses of whatever the hell it was that was happening between them. "We can be romantic together or we can be depraved." He paused for effect. "Or we can be both."

She went still. "I'm in trouble."

"Because you're letting me do bad things to you?"

She nodded. "I shouldn't even be here with you."

"It's too late. We already imprinted on each other." Like animals trapped in a mating ritual, he thought. He released her wrists, freeing her from his captivity. "But I'm not holding you hostage. You're here of your own free will."

"Naked and desperate for you? What kind of free will is that?" She snaked her arms around him, and they rolled over in the bed.

He kissed her, tasting the warmth of her lips and making her sigh. When he raised his head and looked into her eyes, she was staring back at him.

"Are you ready to take me inside?" he asked. He was so aroused, so damned eager, he felt as if he might burst.

"Yes. I'm ready."

He grabbed a condom from the nightstand drawer, and she watched him put it on. She had a naughty knack for watching everything he did. He'd never met anyone who excited him more. She'd become his sexual ideal. A nice girl. A good girl.

He thrust into her, and she keened out a moan

and dug her nails into his back. He didn't care if she clawed the crap out of him. He welcomed anything from her. Anything sexual, he thought, anything that made his body run hot.

She matched his rhythm, stroke for lust-driven stroke. They kissed and growled and behaved like the feral beings they'd become. He flipped her over and did her doggy-style. She gripped the posts on the headboard and pushed back against his aggressive thrusts.

Later, he would be romantic with her. Later he would hold her. For now, he just needed to get the fury out of his blood.

He tugged on the end of her braid. Then he went full bore and undid it, making a mess out of her pretty red hair. He glanced up at the paintings above the bed. He wanted to fill his room with artwork just like it, with images that made him think of Mary.

They changed positions again, and Brandon got back on top. He cupped her breasts, intrigued by her nipples. They were ripe and hard, but the color was soft, like the pink dahlias that grew in the garden on his country estate.

He lowered his head to suck on one of her nipples, and she tunneled her fingers through his hair.

They didn't stay that way for long. Soon they were shifting and moaning. She wrapped her legs around him, and he moved in and out, enthralled with having her as his lover.

She was close to coming. He felt her resolve. He

used his fingers to intensify the stimulation, giving them both a quick fix.

Brandon was just as close. As pressure built in his loins, his vision began to blur. His image of Mary was hazy now.

He took her mouth, kissing her roughly and deep. She came then and there, bucking beneath him. He pulled his mouth away from hers. He couldn't concentrate on kissing anymore. Brandon was caught in a kaleidoscope of sex, of carnal desire, of making love with someone who left him clamoring for more. He tossed back his head, his orgasm shattering between them.

Struggling to catch her breath, Mary roamed her hands over Brandon's back. She couldn't feel the claw marks she'd left on his skin, but she suspected they were there.

"I thought you weren't going to hold me captive," she said. He was big and heavy, his heart beating next to hers.

He lifted his head, piercing her with his gaze. "I'm just enjoying the moment."

She wished that he wasn't staring at her. He always made her nervous when he did that. But when didn't he make her nervous? "The moment is over."

He moved onto his side and held her, ever so gently. "The sex is over, but the afterglow is just beginning."

She panicked, counting off the mistakes in her mind. She shouldn't have slept with him and she shouldn't have lost herself so deeply in it, either. "I'm not glowing. Am I?"

"You definitely are. I've never seen a more beautifully tousled woman."

She glanced away, feeling shy and self-conscious. And guilty, so darned guilty. She didn't have the right to be glowing in his arms.

Finally, he sat up and said, "I have to get rid of the condom. But don't go anywhere. Stay right here."

Did he think she was going to dash into the living room, gather her clothes, get dressed and leave before he came back from the bathroom? "I will."

"Promise?"

"Yes." Running off like a coward wasn't going to help.

While he was gone, she fussed with the sheet. The least she could do was cover up. He was probably right about how tousled she was. She doubted that he was accurate about her being beautiful, though. But she wasn't going to argue with him. It was nice being admired.

Frighteningly nice, she thought.

She glanced up and saw Brandon returning from the bathroom. He was still naked, still perfect in every way.

He had an amused expression. "Check you out, with the covers pulled up to your neck. It's a little late for modesty, don't you think?"

She lied. "I was cold from the air-conditioning."

"Do want me to adjust the thermostat?"

"No, it's okay. You can just come back to bed

with me." She wanted to cuddle with him. But she couldn't ignore her fears, either.

He got under the sheet, but he pulled the fabric lower and looser, so they weren't sandwiched in it. "Why do I get the feeling that you're going to say something I'm not going to like?"

"Because I am." She shifted onto her side, facing him so they could converse. "As wonderful as this is, it's not going to last."

"Why do we have to talk about it being over? Why can't we just see how it unfolds?"

"Because we're not right for each other. We come from different backgrounds. We don't have anything in common." She rattled off the same old excuses, everything except the truth. She couldn't bring herself to say that.

"I think we're getting along just fine."

"We've only had a few dates, and we've never been anywhere where our worlds collide. If you took me into your social circle, you'd see what a mess it would be."

"I disagree. Do you know how many of my friends have been telling me I should find a nice girl like you?"

Heaven help her, she thought, and him, too. "What if I'm the wrong kind of nice? What if what we're doing is riskier than it seems?"

"Why? Because you inspire me to buy naughty paintings and talk about kinky sex? I'll admit that my attraction to you is pretty damn primal. But I want to spend time with you in other ways, too, and get to know you better."

"I want to know you better, too." Only she was wrong to want a real relationship with him. She'd come here to end it, not get closer to him. "But I still don't see how it's going to work."

"Let's just try it, okay? Even if it turns out to be the mess you're convinced it'll be, at least we gave it a shot."

She nuzzled against him, his body strong and solid next to hers. "You make it sound so easy."

"Everything doesn't have to be difficult. Besides, I'm the peacekeeper, remember? That's what I do."

The peacekeeper who'd filed a restraining order against her mother. "Can lawyers be trusted, Brandon?"

He smoothed her tangled hair. "What?"

"The T-shirt you were wearing earlier said that I should trust you."

"I wasn't wearing that as a message for you. It's just a novelty shirt that Tommy gave me. I have tons of them with funny sayings on them."

"So I should trust you?"

He kept smoothing her hair. "Have I done something to you, something that makes you question my integrity?"

"No." He hadn't done anything to her, but there were still the wrongdoings against her mom. "If you damaged someone unknowingly, would you regret it?"

"Of course." He frowned at her. "Wouldn't you?"

"Yes." She moved a little closer, absorbing his warmth, his strength. Her decency had been on the line since she'd met him, but his seemed intact. There was nothing untrustworthy about him, not as far as she could tell. "I'm sorry if I've been saying weird things. I do that sometimes." She didn't know how else to explain her ramblings, but at least he wasn't frowning anymore.

A few silent seconds later, he asked, "Will you spend the weekend with me?"

The change of topic made her blink. "I didn't bring anything with me. I can't wear the same clothes every day. I'd need my toiletries, too."

"I can take you to your apartment tonight, and you can throw an overnight bag together."

"I can run home myself."

He squinted. "As long as you don't ditch me."

"I won't." She intended to come back.

They'd already made love, with tender feelings between them. It wouldn't solve anything to disappear.

For her, the romantic damage had already been done.

By the time Mary returned to her apartment, Alice was home and dressed for bed. The dark makeup was gone and her normally spiked hair was flat, making her look younger than her nineteen years. Even her pajamas were kid-like, with cartoon characters on them.

Mary had hoped to leave her sister a note or send her a text, but now she had to deal with it in person.

After Alice followed Mary into her room, she told her that she was spending the weekend with Brandon. "I went to his house to end it. But then I got caught up in my attraction to him. That's probably no surprise to you. You've been saying all along that I wanted to sleep with him." She took a hurried breath and continued. "Regardless of how long my affair with him lasts, I'm not going to tell him who I am. He's never going to know that we set out to dupe him." No more revenge. For Mary, this was becoming real.

Alice clenched her jaw, disgust flashing in her eyes. "So you're just going to be his adoring little lover and never say anything when it's over? What's the stupid point of that?"

Mary sat on the edge of the bed, which was covered by her old chenille bedspread. "I don't want to hurt him. I don't want him to hate me later, either. It's just better for everyone involved to keep the truth hidden."

"Seriously? You're protecting him, after what he did to Mama?"

"I don't think he did it on purpose. In fact, I'm certain now that he didn't. He's a good person. I'm sure of it."

"And what if you're wrong and he's as conniving as his dad? You're just going to let him and Kirby get away with destroying our family?"

"I told you from the start that I had doubts about Brandon being like Kirby."

"You're so naive."

"I'm just going with my gut."

Alice heaved a noisy sigh. "And now you're falling for Brandon. Even though you said you never would."

"I can't help it." Mary winced, her guilt growing. Feeling much too anxious, she picked at a loose thread on the bedspread. "It all just happened so fast."

"Well, you know what? I can still get my revenge. I can spill the beans and tell him who you are."

Mary turned livid. She'd been nothing but loyal to her sister, caring for her their entire lives. And this was how she was being repaid? "I can't believe you're threatening me."

Alice scoffed like a school-yard bully. "And I can't believe you're choosing him over me and Mama."

"Okay. I get it. You're upset that I care about him. But, please, don't tell him. It'll rip my heart out if you go behind my back and do that."

"Really? Well, he might be the one who ends up ripping your heart out, not me. I know you think he's a good guy, but he's still Kirby's devoted son. No matter how kind he seems, he still has it in his genetics to hurt you."

Mary didn't want to think about anyone hurting anyone. "Just give me your word that you won't betray me and tell him who I am."

"Fine. Whatever."

Alice stormed out of the room, leaving Mary alone to pack. But that was okay. Because for now, all she wanted was to return to Brandon.

Seven

Brandon skimmed a hand down Mary's spine, and she sighed at his touch. They were back in his bed, warm and naked.

"I'm glad you didn't ditch me," he said.

"I told you that I wouldn't." But she wasn't going to tell him about the argument she'd had with Alice. Mary had so many secrets, so many things weighing her down. Her life had always been complicated. She'd spent her youth with a depressed mother and a rebellious sister.

She nuzzled closer to Brandon. Cuddling with him felt good.

"Being around you makes me hungry." He took a pretend bite out of her shoulder. "You smell like cookie dough."

"It's my body spray. I used it right before I came back here." She'd also packed it in her overnight bag. "It's vanilla and cinnamon."

"You must smell like that when you're working, too, except from the real thing."

"Yes, I definitely do." She played with his hair, intrigued by the shiny blackness. For now, pieces of it were falling onto his forehead instead of staying slicked back the way it normally was. She knew he was fascinated by her hair, too, particularly given the way he'd undid her braid earlier.

"Are you tired?" he asked.

She shook her head. She was too exhilarated to be sleepy. She glanced at the clock and saw how late it was. "Are you?"

"Not in the least."

"I'll bet you're not even normally home on Friday nights."

"Not usually, no. There was a gathering I was supposed to attend this evening, but I didn't go. I was hoping that you'd call or come over, and you did."

Curious about the social engagement he'd skipped, she asked, "What kind of gathering was it?"

"A party at a friend's house. He's the architect who designed this building. He and his wife invite me to all of their get-togethers. I have a lot of married friends. I guess it comes with the thirtysomething territory."

She sent him a silly look. "You mean the almost-forty territory?"

He laughed, rolled his eyes. "Easy for you to say, Ms. Twenty-Five and Hardly Been Kissed."

"I never said I'd hardly been kissed. I just said that I only had one boyfriend and that he didn't matter as much as he should have. But I'm never going to describe you as someone who didn't matter." He mattered far too much. "You'll be the one who gave me amazing sex."

He grinned. "Now that works for my ego." As his grin faded, he asked, "Who was the other guy? Will you tell me something about him?"

She considered what to say and how much to share. Then she realized she didn't have anything to hide, at least not where her former boyfriend was concerned. "His name was Jim, and he was the assistant manager at the bakery where I worked in Oklahoma."

"So what was it about him that didn't matter as much as it should have?"

"I just didn't feel as strongly for him as I should have. He was nice and easy to be around. But something was missing between us."

"Where is he now?"

"He still works at the same bakery. He's not an overly ambitious guy. The last I heard, he was dating someone new."

"And now you are, too." He spoke softly. "You and me and the amazing sex."

She thought about the different positions he'd had her in, bending and shaping her to his will. She thought about the romantic way he'd held her afterward, too. "I'm glad you asked me to spend the weekend with you."

"Me, too. Do you want to see my other house tomorrow? We can bring Cline and let him run around. There's lots of acreage for him to play on."

"I'd love to see it." She wanted to make the most of her time with him.

"We can stay there tomorrow instead of coming back here. This might sound odd, but I've never spent the night with anyone at that house. Of course, I rarely stay there myself. The master suite has a huge four-poster bed. My decorator picked it out." He adopted a dastardly expression. "I could totally tie you up in it."

She kicked him under the covers. She assumed he was kidding. Or hoped he was. "That's not funny."

"Then why are you laughing?"

"I'm not." She was smiling like an idiot who didn't know any better. "It's just weird that I inspire bad things in you."

"I think we should do something bad right now."

Her pulse zoomed straight to the V between her legs. "Like what?"

He sat up and reached for his clothes. "Go out for ice cream. There's a fast-food joint nearby that makes the best milkshakes."

Mary leaned on her side to watch him to put his Trust me, I'm a Lawyer T-shirt back on. "That was sneaky."

He zipped his jeans, smiling all the while. "So sue me."

Her mind whirred back to when she and Alice had hoped to sue his father. But this wasn't a good time to think about that.

She hastily said, "I do like milkshakes. Strawberry is my favorite."

"Then get dressed, and let's go."

She obliged him, and they left the loft.

They stepped into the elevator and the door closed, but he didn't push the button that would take them to the bottom floor. He pressed her against the wall instead, kissing her senseless.

While they kissed, while everything inside Brandon went rough and hot, he roamed his hands all over Mary, eager to make his elevator fantasy come true.

When he tore his mouth away from hers, he said, "You can leave your dress on. But you need to take off your panties."

She removed her undies and tucked them into his pants' pocket. "Does this mean we're not going out for ice cream?"

He laughed at her fake innocence. She was turning him on but good. Her panties were burning a hole in his pocket. He just might keep them as a trophy from their affair. "We can still get the milkshakes when we're done."

She bit down on her bottom lip. "Done with what?"

"As if you don't know." In his other pocket he had a condom. He'd stashed it there while she'd been getting dressed. He undid his jeans. He was already hard. He handed her the packet. "Do you want to do the honors?"

She fumbled with the package. "I've never actually been the one to…"

Now her innocence seemed real. Or her inexperience or whatever. Brandon was too damned aroused to wait it out. "No worries. I'll do it." He took it from her.

He donned the protection, yanked up her dress and thrust into her. She gasped and pulled him closer.

They went mad, frenzied and wild, groping through their clothes and kissing. Because he was so much taller, he had to bend his knees and lift her into a position that gave him deeper access.

She moaned, so hot, so vocal.

He liked that she was wearing the same dress from before. He liked how sweet and wholesome it looked on her. Even while they were having lust-driven sex, she still seemed sweet.

Her cookie dough scent was driving him crazy, too.

She clung to him, and he stroked her with his fingers, making her wetter.

"Come with me." He needed a release so damned badly, but he wanted her to have one, too.

She dug her nails into his shoulders, pressing them into his shirt. She'd scratched his skin earlier, and he'd loved every feral second of it.

"Come with me," he said again, nearly growling the words into her ear.

She dug her nails deeper and harder. "I am. I will."

Damn straight, he thought. He felt a shiver rising up in her body and taking over.

Her orgasm triggered his, giving him the release he'd been waiting for, sensation slamming into sensation, pressure building into pressure.

Cripes, it was good.

When it was over, he put his forehead against hers, and they both sucked air into their lungs.

"Where have you been all of my life?" he asked, teasing her with a clichéd line.

She retrieved her panties from his pocket. "When you were twenty, I was eleven, maybe twelve. So for most of your life, I was a kid. And when you were a kid, I wasn't even born yet."

"Listen to you, being so literal." So much for him keeping her underwear. She was already putting her panties back on. He glanced down at himself. He had the condom to deal with. But it was what it was. He removed the rubber and tied it off.

"Elevator safety," she said.

He raised his eyebrows. "Are you making a safe sex joke?"

"After what we just did? Can you blame me?"

"No, I can't say that I do." He pushed the button, and the elevator descended.

Once they were in the parking structure, he tossed the condom into a nearby trash can.

They got into his car, and he asked, "Will you come to Texas with me in August, to Matt and Libby's wedding?" He knew it was a random question, but now that they were lovers, he didn't want to attend the festivities alone.

She buckled her seat belt. "You want to bring me to something like that, with all of your family there?" She sounded panicked.

"My family isn't going to rip you apart. We're not a pack of wolves."

She didn't look as if she believed him.

Damn, he thought. She was a tough case. He sighed and said, "Just think about it, okay?"

She stared out the windshield. "It's just a lot for me to take in right now."

He fired up the engine and pulled out of the parking lot. "We agreed to give this a shot, Mary. To continue dating and seeing each other."

"I know. But I didn't think that it would include your brother's wedding."

He didn't see what the big deal was. He'd brought a date to Tommy's wedding, too. "I just want us to dance, to sip champagne, to have a little fun."

"I know," she said again, without turning to look at him. "But it's still so new and overwhelming, being with someone like you."

He was overwhelmed being with her, too. And as elusive as she was, he would probably have hell to pay, trying to keep their affair afloat.

He pulled into the drive-through at the burger joint and placed their orders, then they sat in the car as they drank their shakes: chocolate for him and strawberry for her.

"How long were you with Jim?" he asked. Typically, he didn't care about a woman's romantic past. But with Mary, everything seemed to matter.

She shifted in her seat. "We were together for six months."

"Were you always threatening to break it off with him?"

"No. But I was just used to him, I guess."

"So when are you going to get used to me?" He leaned in her direction, bumping her shoulder and forcing her to feel his flustered affection.

She turned all the way toward him. "I'm sorry if I'm being difficult. But it's hard not to think about how high society you are. Or how famous your family is. That's tough for an average girl like me."

"You're far from average." She was the most complicated woman he'd ever known.

She reached up to touch his face. Her hand was cold from holding her milkshake. "I never expected to get this close to you. It's an emotional process for me."

For him, too, but in a different way than it was for her. He was anxious to bring her into his life, and she was keeping him on the fringes of hers.

She removed her hand from his cheek. "Sitting here with you almost makes it seem as if we tumbled back in time."

"Like teenagers from the 1950s on their way home from a sock hop?"

She nodded. "Where did you go to high school?"

"It was a prep school, not too far from here. I was our class president and the valedictorian. Tommy attended public school. He wasn't interested in a private education. It was too uppity for him. Or that's what he said, anyway. But I think he just wanted to go to the same school as Sophie."

"My high school was in a rough part of town, so we didn't have any rich kids there." She leaned back against her seat. "But you probably already deduced that I grew up poor."

"Yes." But as to how poor, he didn't have a clue. "I can't even begin to know what that was like for you." He had wealthy parents who gave him whatever he wanted, whenever he wanted it. Of course, mostly all he and Tommy ever wanted was for their bleary-eyed dad to get clean and sober.

"We struggled to make ends meet. But some of the kids I grew up with were worse off than us."

"When did your parents die, Mary? I know you don't like to talk about it, but—"

"Please, let's not ruin this night by going there." She glanced at him, a pained expression on her face. "I want to have happy memories of being here with you."

"I'm sorry." He shouldn't have pushed those boundaries. It was only their first weekend together. "I can be aggressive sometimes."

"It must be the lawyer in you."

"Yeah." But it was his interest in her, too, and how strongly she affected him. "How about if we listen to some music?"

"That sounds nice."

"You can go through my playlist and choose."

"Thanks." She scanned his device and picked some old country tunes.

They sat quietly, enjoying the music and their milkshakes. After a short while, he asked, "Have you ever heard Tommy's song, 'The Urban Name Game,' where he pokes fun at some of the definitions in the urban dictionary?"

"No, I don't think I have."

"It's not one of his bigger hits. But he thinks the over-the-top meanings people make up for their names on that site are funny, so that's what inspired him to write it. We can play his song later if you want to hear it. He was going to use my name in it, but I told him I would kick his ass if he did."

"What are some of the definitions of your name that caught his attention?"

"That Brandon is an awesome guy, smart and funny and ridiculously charming. That just knowing someone named Brandon is considered lucky, and it might even help you win the lottery. You can't go wrong with Brandon. Even when he is being a jerk, people are quick to forgive him."

She sent him a wry look. "So you're an awesome jerk with the power to bring luck?"

He laughed at the foolishness of it. "I wonder what some of yours are." He grabbed his phone and got on the site. "Ah, here we are." He scanned the first few entries and raised his eyebrows. "Apparently Mary is a kind and caring girl who will warm your heart. She's also highly committed and will be loyal to only you. Once you get together with Mary, you'll want to keep her forever."

She acted smug. "That sounds about right."

"Oh, sure, the perfect woman." Just for the hell of it, he kissed her, slipping his tongue into her mouth and making everything but the taste of her go away.

When they separated, she said, "I like it when you do that."

"I like it, too." He studied her in the shadowy light. "Do you know the true origin of your name?"

She nodded. "In Hebrew it means 'wish for child.' But it also means 'sea of bitterness' and 'rebellion.' I always figured that the Virgin Mary was the reason for the 'wish-for-child' thing. I don't know about the rest of it." She set her drink down. "What does Brandon mean for real?"

Nothing as interesting as Mary, he thought. "A hill covered with broom."

She cracked a smile. "The kind you sweep with?"

"No, smarty." He tried to seem indignant, but he thought it was funny, too. "A flowering shrub."

"I knew what you meant." She gave a soft sigh. "It's actually a pretty visual, if you think about it."

"You're the pretty visual." He kissed her one more time, before he took her back to his loft and back to his bed.

Mary spent the following day with Brandon at his country estate. The redbrick, two-story home sat on four acres and had six bedrooms, seven baths, a swimming pool and a gazebo.

The whole place was light and airy with dome-shaped windows and rounded archways. The floors were wood and the fireplaces trimmed in marble. Everywhere that Mary looked, on tables, shelves and walls, were stunning pieces of art. But Brandon had already told her that he used the house to store and display the bulk of his collection.

After he completed the tour and escorted her outside to sit by the pool, one of the caretakers, an older woman with a friendly smile, brought them lemonade.

Once she was gone, Brandon said to Mary, "You can see how much Cline enjoys being here."

"Definitely." The dog was playing in the yard, racing around in the grass. "It's funny that you take him for walks in the park every Sunday when you could just bring him here."

"I like going to the park. It makes me feel free, to go out in public and just be with my dog. When I was a kid, I used to wonder what it would be like to come from a regular family. My childhood was like a circus, with all of the fans hanging around at the gate at Kirbyville. The paparazzi were a huge factor, too."

She reached for her glass, which was artfully garnished with fresh mint and lemon wedges. "Do you think Matt's wedding will be a circus?" There was a part of her that wanted to go, to be there with Brandon. But how was she supposed to face his father, knowing what he'd done to her mother?

He replied, "It'll be a private ceremony on Matt's

recreational ranch, with plenty of security in case the media tries to crash it. So I don't think it'll be a problem." He caught her gaze. "Are you reconsidering taking the trip with me?"

"I don't know." She was already feeling like a stranger in a strange land, so how could she subject herself to his entire family? Still, traveling with Brandon sounded romantic.

"If you decide to come, it'll be four days. The first two will be wedding stuff, and the last two we'll be on our own. We'd be staying in one of the guest cabins on the ranch. There are lots of things to do— hiking, fishing, horseback riding." He added, "I'm not a cowboy like Matt and Tommy, but I grew up around horses."

"So you like to ride?"

"Definitely. I do Western and English. I played a little polo in college."

That didn't surprise her. He was a Harvard man, and it seemed like something he would do. "I've only been riding a few times, and that was when I was younger." Mama used to take her and Alice to a rental stable, but it wasn't a luxury they could regularly afford.

"Did you enjoy it?" he asked.

"Yes, very much." But she couldn't tell him about her mother's love of horses and how much it meant to Mama to give her daughters those experiences. Mary even had some old photos of her and Alice astride the rental ponies. But that was before the Kirby fiasco, before Mama got so depressed.

She cleared her mind and glanced around. "Is this property zoned for horses?"

"Yes, but I don't see the point of getting any, not unless I stayed here more often. I can ride at Tommy's whenever I want to."

"Are you and Tommy going to be in Matt's wedding?"

He nodded. "He asked us to be his groomsmen."

Mary went quiet. If she'd met Brandon under different circumstances, if his father hadn't hurt her mother, if Brandon hadn't filed the restraining order, this affair would be so much easier. But as it was, it shouldn't be happening at all.

"You've got that look," he said.

She glanced up. "What look?"

"As if you're considering ending it with me again."

"I'm not." But she should be, she thought. "Really, I'm not." She wasn't ready to let him go. She made a grand gesture, trying to focus on something else. "This really is a wonderful house. It's too bad you don't get more use out of it."

"Why don't we go for a swim?" He smiled. "Cline loves to swim, too, if you don't mind sharing the pool with a big, smelly dog."

She laughed. "He isn't smelly."

"He will be when he gets wet. But that'll just give us an excuse to shower together." He smiled again, sexier this time. "Without the dog."

"Okay," she said, scooting her chair closer to his. "I'm game." She'd seen the shower in the master bath, and it was a huge glass enclosure with a variety of water jets. She could only imagine how glorious it was going to feel. Brandon was fast becoming the lover of her dreams. Dreams she didn't even know she had. "I didn't bring a swimsuit, though. It hadn't occurred to me that I might need one."

"There are tons of brand-new suits in the pool house. I'm sure there'll be some in your size." He shrugged. "My caretakers provide them, just in case I have guests."

"Thank you for inviting me here." As mixed up as everything was, he had a way of making her feel better.

This beautiful man that she was deceiving.

Eight

Swimming with the dog was fun, and the shower with Brandon was heavenly, just as Mary had assumed it would be.

The main fixture poured water over them like a waterfall. The rest of the jets kept steady streams shooting at them from different directions. Luxury at its finest, she thought, with a tall, tanned, blue-eyed attorney. Before he'd come into her life, she couldn't have imagined a scenario like this if she'd tried.

He washed her hair with his shampoo and conditioner, and she inhaled the crisp fragrance. She liked him using his products on her. She liked everything about this weekend with him. Everything except the lies she was keeping. She hoped their affair ended mutually, during a time when both of them were ready to let go, and her secret could fade into oblivion.

Brandon finished washing her hair and spun her around to kiss her. She latched on to him as if there was no tomorrow, hating herself for what she was doing to him. The more time she spent with him, the more convinced she was that he was a kind and caring person. That he hadn't hurt her mother deliberately. That it had been all Kirby's doing. But Brandon loved his father, just as she'd loved her mother. Nothing good could ever come of this.

He deepened the kiss, and her mind went blank. She reached between his legs and stroked him, making him big and hard. She ran her thumb over the tip, moving in little circles, and he shuddered.

Wanting to give him the same kind of pleasure he'd already given her, she ended the kiss and dropped to her knees.

He looked down at her, and their gazes met and held. He shut off the side jets to keep her from getting drenched, but the waterfall fixture was still running, creating a sensual ambience.

She took him in her mouth, and he played with the wet strands of her hair. She imagined how she must look to him, this nice girl that she supposedly was, taking him all the way to the back of her throat.

She enhanced his experience with flicks of her tongue, and he rocked his hips. The hands in her hair tightened. She felt powerful, knowing that he was having trouble containing himself. But she felt dominated by him, too.

It was a feeling she liked. A feeling that aroused her.

He growled her name, and it echoed through the spray of water. She increased the rhythm, using her hands and her mouth.

Right before he came, he tried to pull away. But she tugged him closer, letting him know that she wanted him to spill into her. So that's what he did, in the midst of rising steam and splashing water, with his stomach muscles jumping and his breathing short and shaky.

Afterward, he staggered, and she eased back. But she didn't get up off her knees. She touched herself, running her hands over her breasts and working her way down, pressing her fingers between her thighs. Mary needed to come, too.

Brandon didn't intervene. By now, he'd recovered from his orgasm. He remained at his full height and watched her. Clearly, he was enjoying the show.

She closed her eyes and let the sensation of performing for him sweep her away.

Finally, when she was sated, she climbed to her feet and turned off the waterfall. Their sexy shower was over.

They left the enclosure and dried off with towels and heat lamps.

Brandon said, "That was incredible." He put his jeans on. They'd both brought clothes into the bathroom. "But how am I supposed to ever be with anyone else after that?"

She got dressed, too. "I'd rather not think about you being with someone else."

"Good. Because I'm hanging on to you as long as I can."

"You're turning me into someone new." Someone far more daring than she'd ever expected to be. She moved closer to him. "I should be blushing."

"Sometimes you blush. I like both sides of you, the good girl and the bad. It's tough to make up my mind which one excites me more."

She nuzzled against him. "I think I'm becoming more bad than good." But for now her heart was pounding, relentlessly, right next to his.

On Sunday morning, Mary and Brandon took Cline to the park. As they strolled beside the river, she envisioned spending every weekend together. But she knew that wasn't possible.

Brandon stopped to let Cline sniff a tree. "I have to go out of town next week for work. I have an important client in Vegas, so I go there fairly often."

"I thought your parents and Tommy were your most important clients." She knew that he specialized in entertainment law because he wanted to represent his family.

The family he protected, she thought. She'd tried to protect hers, too, but she'd failed where Brandon had succeeded. Her family was a mess, and his was a success.

He replied, "Mom and Dad and Tommy will always come first. But I'm still loyal to my other clients."

As well he should be, she thought. He'd built his practice on some of the biggest names in the music industry. But without his family, he wouldn't have made those connections. He'd grown up around celebrities.

He resumed walking, and she fell into step with him. If only she wasn't developing such strong feelings for him. If only he wasn't burrowing inside her.

"My dad wants to start dating again," he said.

She started. "What? With who?"

"With whoever he is attracted to, I guess. We didn't talk about how he plans to meet someone new. Mostly he just wanted to run it past me. He hasn't been with anyone since he's been clean and sober, and he's getting lonely for companionship. He spoke to Tommy about it, but my brother isn't too keen on the idea."

Her heart thumped. "And you are?"

"It's not my decision to make. But I told Dad that I'd support him. Tommy isn't convinced that our old man has changed, at least not where females are concerned. But I think Dad is respectful of women now."

She tried to curb her distain, but some of it came out anyway. "What if Tommy is right?"

He frowned at her. "You don't approve of my father, do you?"

She glanced away. "I don't even know him."

"But it's obvious that you don't like the way he was portrayed in his book. You made that clear on our first date."

"I just don't like the way he treated his wife and children." And she especially couldn't bear the way he'd treated her mom. After his betrayal, Mama was afraid that all of Nashville would find out that she'd been accused of harassing one of the biggest country stars on the planet. Her dream of making it in that industry had been completely crushed.

"Are you reluctant to attend Matt's wedding because you're uncomfortable about meeting my dad?" Brandon asked.

At this point she couldn't find it within herself to lie. "Yes, he's a big part of it."

"I know that his past isn't very reassuring, but he's taking responsibility for it now. If you met him, I think you'd like him. Sophie gets along great with him and so does Libby. He even walked Sophie down the aisle when she and Tommy got married. No matter how often Dad and Tommy fight, they still have a bond that can't be denied."

Mary missed the bond she'd once had with her mother. She and Alice still had Mama's songbook tucked away in a safe deposit box. For them, it was her most important belonging.

He said, "I'm sorry if I keep pushing you toward my family. I just really want you to go to the wedding with me."

"It's still a month away." By now June was gone, and they were in the midst of July. "Maybe I'll be able to handle it by then."

"I hope so." Behind him, the river was dappled with sunlight, specks of gold dancing on the water.

The setting was too pretty for her to be stressing about Kirby, she thought. But Brandon's father was never far from her mind. "Will you call me when you get back from Las Vegas?"

He looked longingly into her eyes. "Definitely. I can't wait to see you again."

She fought the sudden fuzziness in her brain. Would they ever get enough of each other? Would this feeling ever end?

"I can't wait to see you again, either." To touch him, to feel his naked body against hers. But it was more than just the sex. She felt safe and warm when she was with Brandon, which made no sense.

Mary was confused, as usual. Even Cline was cocking his silvery head at her, as if he was trying to figure her out. Then again, the dog always seemed to sense her emotions.

And no one made Mary more emotional than Brandon.

Mary bustled around her apartment, plumping pillows on the sofa and making sure everything looked as nice as it possibly could. Brandon had just gotten back from his trip and was on his way over, directly from the airport.

This was a big step for her, letting him see her home. It just felt more personal than her going to his houses. But he'd asked if he could stop by, saying that he had some important news he wanted to share.

"Maybe I should hang out for a while," Alice said.

"No." Mary shook her head. "You said you had things to do today." Alice was supposed to be gone before he arrived.

"But I want to meet him." Her sister plopped down on the sofa, scattering the plumped pillows.

"Not now." She couldn't deal with introducing Alice to Brandon, and especially not today. "You know how nervous I am already."

"Maybe you're just afraid that I'll blow the whistle on you."

"You promised that you wouldn't." But was she concerned about being able to trust Alice? Yes, heaven help her, she was. "Please, just go run your errands."

"I'll leave if you agree to invite Brandon over for dinner this weekend. We can cook for him together. We can make it a cozy little get-together."

It sounded like a disaster to Mary, the worst idea in history. "And if I refuse to invite him?"

Alice put her feet on the coffee table. She even clicked her boot heels together. "Then I might be forced to break my promise and tell him the truth."

Mary glared at her. She was being blackmailed by her baby sister. Still, what choice did she have but to give in? Alice had the advantage. "Fine. I'll arrange for you to meet him. But you have to keep my secret. You have to swear on Mama's grave."

Her sister scoffed. "Now there's a low blow. Mama doesn't even have a grave."

Their mother had been cremated, with her ashes scattered in the Oklahoma wind. They hadn't been able to afford a funeral or a traditional burial. But Mama would have preferred being part of the elements, anyway. Mary didn't regret the choice they'd made. "Just swear it."

"All right. I swear. But it seems weird that you're so adamant about lying to him. If you never tell him who you are, he won't understand what went wrong. If you care about him, then don't you at least owe him that much?"

Mary squinted at her sister. "What are you doing? Trying to use some sort of reverse psychology on me?"

"I'm just stating the facts."

"What facts? That you want him to know that we plotted against him? That you want to see him get hurt?" She didn't trust Alice's motives, not one iota. "He'll be better off never knowing who I am."

"If you say so." Alice stood, grabbed her long-fringed purse and stomped over to the front door. "But don't forget to invite him to dinner and tell him how much I'm looking forward to meeting him." She batted her lashes before she left, making an even bigger mockery of their conversation. When she was a kid she used to make ugly faces when she was being a brat. Now she was being all pretty about it.

Once she was gone, Mary righted the pillows on the sofa. She hoped Brandon's news wasn't about the wedding. She'd already been losing far too much sleep over that.

About twenty minutes later, Brandon arrived. He was gorgeous as ever, in a gray pullover and black slacks.

Mary showed him around the apartment, and he lingered in her bedroom.

"So this is where you sleep," he said, stating the obvious.

She nodded. The old chenille spread had been passed down from her grandmother. Mama had used it when she was young, too. Everything was done in pastels, including her furniture.

She watched him walk over to her dresser. He didn't have far to go. The room was small and crowded. He lifted a cupcake-shaped candle from her dresser and studied it. "This is cute. It suits you." He turned to look at her bed. She had three stuffed animals, two bears and a bunny, on it. "Are these from when you were a kid?" he asked.

"Yes." The manner in which he was scrutinizing everything was making her uncomfortable. Suddenly she feared that he knew who she was. That he'd found out somehow and was mocking her with his "cute" comments. Was it possible that Alice had gone behind her back and told him? She could have gotten his number from Mary's phone.

No, that didn't make sense. Why would Alice have

threatened to reveal Mary's identity if she'd already done it? And why would she have insisted on inviting Brandon to dinner?

"What are their names?" he asked.

She blinked. "What?"

He gestured. "The stuffed animals."

Oh, right. Her old toys. "The bunny is Beanie and the bears are Daisy and Dilly."

He moved toward the bed and sat on the edge of it. He even picked up Beanie and stroked its frayed ears.

"What's going on?" she asked, needing to know what his agenda was. "What did you want to talk to me about?"

His face lit up. "I came here to tell you about Zoe."

She relaxed, grateful that his news seemed positive. "What about her?"

He bounced Beanie on his lap. "She arrived two days ago, while I was still in Vegas, but they just brought her home today. Sophie had her in a private birthing center, so they were able to keep it out of the press. Tommy plans to make a formal announcement and release some pictures. But he wants the family to meet her first. I haven't seen her yet. But I intend to make her acquaintance, just as soon as I leave here."

"That's nice, Brandon." She could see how excited he was.

"I was wondering if you'd come with me."

Oh, no. "What about your dad?" This sounded worse than the wedding. Or just as bad. "I need more time to meet him." Or she needed to not meet him at all, she thought.

"Dad won't be there. My parents were already at Tommy's place this morning, helping Sophie and the baby get settled in. They were at the clinic when she was born, too, so they've had lots of time with her. Matt and Libby and Chance are flying in tomorrow. Tommy is trying to keep everyone's visits separate so Sophie won't get too worn out."

"So it'll just be you and me?"

"Yep. Just us."

"I don't have anything to bring." There was always something to fret about, it seemed. "You already gave them a beautiful piece of art."

"I always give people art."

"And normally I bake for people."

"So you can bake for them another time. Tommy and Sophie will understand that this was a rushed visit. Just come with me," he implored her.

"Okay, I will." She wanted to support Brandon. And since Kirby wouldn't be around, she didn't have to panic about running into him. "Speaking of family, my sister wants you to come over for dinner this weekend. She's interested in meeting you."

"Really?" He put Beanie down. "Oh, that's cool. I'd like to meet her, too."

"She might not be that friendly. I think she's jealous that I'm seeing you." Mary figured it wouldn't hurt to warn him that Alice might behave strangely.

"Do you think it would help if I brought her a gift?"

"After you just told me not to worry about bringing something to Tommy and Sophie?"

"That's not the same thing. You just said that Alice is jealous that you're dating me."

"I know. But it isn't necessary to bring her a present." Short of millions of dollars, she doubted that he would be able to buy Alice's affection. And even then, her sister would probably still hate him. Mary went over and sat beside him on the bed. "I think it's better to just let Alice be her difficult self."

"I'm just glad that she wants to meet me. And I'm especially happy that you're going with me today."

"I like babies." But she wasn't thrilled with how much she needed Brandon. She struggled with that every day.

He leaned in to kiss her, and she wished for the umpteenth time that his father had never ruined her mother.

When Brandon broke the kiss, he said, "I can come to dinner on Saturday. Does that day work for you, or would Sunday be better?"

"Saturday is fine. I'm sure that will be fine with Alice, too, since it was her idea."

"I've been keeping my schedule clear for you. There was a ball I could've attended this weekend, but I declined the invitation. I don't want to go alone, and I didn't think you would've agreed to go with me." He paused, sighed. "I'd love to sweep you off to a fancy ball and introduce you to my friends. But

I'm already concerned about scaring you away. I'm trying to have this affair on your terms."

"I appreciate that you're putting my feelings first." Except for the part where he wanted her to accept his father—the very thing that scared her most.

Tommy and Sophie lived in one of the biggest, grandest custom-built mansions in Nashville. Once Mary and Brandon passed through the security gate, she worried about what she'd gotten herself into. Brandon fit naturally into the opulent setting, but Mary felt like a little church mouse. She dusted off the fabric of her plain white skirt, wishing that she were prettier and more sophisticated and everything else that Brandon's other lovers were.

He glanced over at her. "Are you okay?"

"I was just thinking about what you said earlier about wishing you could take me to one of your fancy balls and introduce me to your friends. You're right that it would scare me."

He parked in the big circular driveway and reached across the console for her hand. "Maybe in time, my lifestyle won't seem so daunting to you."

"I don't even know how to dance."

"You mean waltz or country dance?"

"Waltz. I can two-step." She'd been reared on down-home music. Her mother used to dance her and Alice all over their ratty little apartment. Mama had even worked at a record store when she was younger—the type that barely existed anymore.

Later, she'd worked at an insurance company, doing boring office stuff.

Brandon interrupted her thoughts. "Waltzing isn't that much different than two-stepping. I can teach you."

"It looks different on TV."

"On those dance competition shows? That doesn't count. We wouldn't be competing for a prize. It would just be two people swaying in each other's arms. You and I are good together that way."

Her cheeks went warm. He was obviously talking about sex. "We better go inside and see the baby." They certainly couldn't stay here, with him saying sensually charged things to her.

They exited the car, and she forced herself to breathe, as deeply and calmly as she could.

A woman with salt-and-pepper hair answered the door. Mary soon learned that her name was Dottie and that she managed the household staff and kept the estate running.

Dottie gave Brandon a big warm hug. She was kind and friendly to Mary, too, making the moment easier.

"Just wait until you see Zoe," Dottie said to Brandon. "You're going to fall in love with your niece."

He grinned. "I don't doubt that I will."

"Oh, and the painting you bought for Zoe is just the most adorable thing."

"Thanks. Mary helped me pick it out."

"Well, you have an eye for art, my dear." Dottie patted her hand. "For men, too," she mock whispered.

Mary couldn't think of an appropriate response, but she didn't have to. Brandon quickly said, "Hey. I heard that."

The older lady laughed. "You were meant to."

He laughed, too. "When are you going to leave Tommy and work for me?"

"Never," she replied, just as jokingly. "That brother of yours couldn't get along without me. But seriously, he and Sophie and the baby..." She sighed, quite dreamily. "They're perfect together." She nudged Brandon and Mary toward a luxurious staircase with polished wood banisters. "Go on up and see them. They're waiting for you."

Mary noticed a clear glass elevator in a secluded section of the massive entryway. She was glad they weren't using that. She didn't want to think about elevators right now. It would only remind her of what she and Brandon had done in the one at his loft.

The nursery was on the second floor. It overflowed with the ribbons, lace and bows that Mary expected to see. Even the crib was a lavish sight to behold, designed for a princess.

And Tommy and his family? They were perfect together, just as Dottie had said they were.

Tommy looked exactly like he did in his music videos: tall and decidedly Western, with stylishly messy light brown hair and a crooked smile. Sophie was a petite brunette, beaming with motherhood. She sat in an overstuffed rocker on the other side of the room, with the baby in her arms.

"You must be Mary," Tommy said, before Brandon got a chance to introduce her. "It's nice to meet you. That's my wife, Sophie, over there, and our brand-new daughter."

Mary smiled at him and nodded to Sophie, who gave her a gentle nod in return.

"What a special time this is for you," she said to Tommy.

"It's amazing." He turned toward Brandon and they hugged, clapping each other on the back. Then Tommy asked his brother, "Do you want to hold Zoe?"

"God, yes." A grin stretched across Brandon's face. "I've been waiting to get my hands on that kid."

Tommy gestured for Mary to join them. They headed for Sophie and the baby, and the new mother transferred her child into Brandon's arms, showing him what to do.

"She's beautiful." He held the infant carefully, protecting her neck and head. "Just like I knew she would be."

Zoe was a darling baby, Mary thought, with her thick cap of dark hair, hazel eyes and rosy cheeks. She had a cute little expression on her face, as if she was trying to focus on how handsome her uncle was.

Mary was focusing on the same thing. He looked incredible with the pink bundle in his arms. She glanced over at Sophie and said, "She looks like you."

"That's what Tommy says. That she's a mirror image of me. But she has his eyes. His change colors sometimes, going from brown to green, then back again. Hers will probably do that, too, depending on her moods."

"I can only imagine how happy you are." Suddenly marriage and babies and nesting with the man you loved sounded like something Mary wanted to try someday. But even as the thought crossed her mind, she went into panic mode. Love and marriage and babies should be the last thing swimming around in her head, especially while she was having an affair with Brandon.

Nine

Brandon and Tommy stood on the balcony attached to the nursery and gazed at the gardens below. They'd stepped outside for a few minutes, giving themselves the opportunity to be alone and marvel over the new life in their family.

"I think that's the first time I ever held a newborn," Brandon said, and glanced over his shoulder at the glass door behind him. Zoe was inside with the women. After he'd held her, he'd given her back to Sophie.

"I know. It's amazing, isn't it? How tiny she is, with all of those little fingers and toes?" Tommy smiled. "It's even more incredible than I thought it would be. Every time I look at her, I could burst."

"The love a parent has for a child is supposed to

be the strongest bond on earth." Brandon was glad that Tommy was getting to experience it. "It's funny, too, because you're the last person any of us expected to have kids."

"And now I want a houseful." His brother furrowed his brow. "I know Mom loved us the way I love Zoe, but do you think Dad felt this way when we were born?"

Brandon wasn't surprised to hear Tommy question their father's feelings for them, not with how uncertain he'd always been about their dad. "He was messed up during that period of his life, but, yeah, I think he loved us the way he was supposed to."

"He didn't love Matt that way."

"Maybe he did and he was just too afraid to admit it. You know how guilty he was about breaking his promise to Mom and having a kid with someone else."

Tommy's expression softened. "Dad is a wonderful grandpa, I'll give him that much. He's over the moon about Zoe. I practically had to kick him and Mom out of here today. They'd both move into Zoe's nursery if they could."

"But you and Sophie will be doing that instead." They'd created a newly designed master suite adjoined to the nursery. They'd added luxurious accommodations for their nanny, too. "Life is good, eh?"

"For me, this is the best it's ever been. I can't wait to watch my daughter grow up, to teach her to be a cowgirl and play music."

Brandon teased him, saying, "I think you'll be wearing frilly hats and having tea parties with her."

Tommy grinned. "If that's what she wants me to do, then I will. You can join us, bro. We can be frilly-hat dudes together."

"Sure. Why not?" Brandon wanted to be a fun-loving uncle. He wanted his niece to be able to count on him. "We should make Dad wear one, too."

His brother laughed. "His will have to be black."

"I'll bet he'd wear pink for Zoe."

Tommy nodded. "Yeah, he probably would." A second later, he sighed and said, "Did Dad tell you he wants to start dating again?"

"Yes, he told me. I encouraged him to give it a try."

"I guess it'll be okay, as long as he never hurts anyone again."

"I don't think he will." Brandon trusted their father to be a better man. "He's been trying so hard to change."

Tommy squinted in the sunlight. "Speaking of dating, I like your new lady. She seems sweet."

"She is." Totally sweet. Totally sexy. "I'm getting hooked on her."

"So I gathered. You wouldn't have brought her here otherwise. I know I probably shouldn't tell you this, but after Sophie and I got together, I was hoping that you'd find someone, too. Sophie warned me not to play matchmaker or try to set you up with anyone. She said that if it was meant to happen, you'd meet the right woman on your own." His brother squinted again. "Do you think that you and Mary might have a future?"

"I don't know. It's a bit complicated." Or a lot complicated, he thought, with how much he'd come to care about her. "She's been cautious since I met her, and after she read Dad's biography, it got worse. She's leery of him."

"Can't say as I blame her. Even he admitted in the book that he treated people like crap."

"He also said how sorry he was. With Mary, it seems as if there could be something more going on, something related to her family. Both of her parents are dead, and she refuses to talk about them. I'm starting to wonder if maybe her father was a womanizer. If he could've been like our dad, and that type of guy leaves her cold. He might've even been abusive to her mother."

"That could account for why she's so sensitive about her parents. And why it's difficult for her to discuss them."

"Yeah, but I can't be sure." Brandon was at a loss to know what Mary's issues were. "I invited her to Matt's wedding, but she's uncomfortable about going."

"She might come around by then."

"She has a younger sister, and I'm going to meet her this weekend. But Mary already warned me that her sister is jealous of our relationship."

"Sounds like you have your work cut out for you."

"I definitely do." Yet even as difficult as it was, his fascination with Mary grew stronger each day.

When he and Tommy returned to the nursery, Mary was holding the baby, rocking the infant as if it was the most natural thing in the world. Zoe kicked her little feet and cooed.

Brandon moved closer, his attraction to Mary spiking even higher. He couldn't force her to talk about her parents, but he wasn't giving up on her, either. He was going to be there, for as long as she wanted him.

On Saturday evening Mary and Alice fixed chicken and dumplings, something Mary had always thought of as comfort food. They also prepared green beans with bacon, sweet peas, mashed potatoes and fried okra. Mary baked corn bread, too. For dessert, she had double-chocolate brownies and strawberry-lemon bars ready to go. She'd made a frozen mint chip pie, as well. All she had to do was take it out of the freezer when it was time to serve it.

Brandon arrived bearing gifts. The wine he'd brought wasn't the problem. But the other things? Holy cow. Apparently it didn't matter that she'd told him not to bring Alice anything. He'd done it anyway. But he'd brought Mary something special, too.

He gave her the fairy painting he'd wanted to buy her from before. Alice's gift was artwork, too: a beautifully framed acrylic that depicted fashion throughout the ages. She seemed impressed by it, even if she was treating Brandon with a cool and critical eye.

"Was it expensive?" Alice asked him, about her painting.

Mary wanted to kick her sister for being so rude. She'd been taught better than that. But Alice obviously didn't care about being well mannered in this situation. Thank goodness Mary had already warned Brandon what to expect.

Either way, he handled Alice just fine. He politely replied, "I'm an art collector, so I always give people the most valuable work I can find. I enjoy buying select pieces for family and friends."

"I'm not your friend," she said. "And we're certainly not family."

"Your sister is my friend, and you two are family. That's reason enough for me."

Alice shifted her booted feet. She was dressed in her fanciest cowpunk attire. "I'm going to look it up online later and see how much it cost."

He laughed a little. "Go right ahead. I won't be offended."

Alice glared at him. "You don't seem like the type who offends easily."

"Neither do you." He gestured to her outfit. "You have an interesting sense of style. My dad wears black all the time, too."

Alice stiffened before she said, "I don't like his music."

"I wasn't implying that you did. But you have the sort of attitude depicted in his songs. Even though he's drawn to gentle-spirited women, he writes about the sassy ones."

Alice narrowed her gaze. "My sister has a gentle spirit. Our mother did, too."

Mary nearly gasped. Was she going to tell Brandon who they were? She'd sworn that she wouldn't. Yet she'd just mentioned their mother.

"I'd love to see a picture of your mom," he said. "I didn't see any photographs last time I was here."

Mary held her breath, praying that her sister didn't betray her and dig out an old snapshot. She felt faint just thinking about it. Did Brandon know what their mom looked like? Would he recognize her?

"We keep her pictures private," Alice replied. "She's gone now. But she was a good person."

He spoke softly. "I'm sorry you and Mary lost her. I haven't lost anyone I'm close to. I don't know what that feels like. But I can see how painful it is for you."

Alice stepped back, putting distance between her and Brandon. Clearly, she didn't want his sympathy. Mary did, though. She wanted to cuddle in his arms and take refuge in his strength. But she wouldn't dare do that in front of Alice.

"We better sit down and eat before everything gets cold," Mary said.

"Thanks for inviting me," Brandon said. "Both of you." He gazed at Alice. "Mary told me it was your idea."

"I just wanted to know who my sister is sleeping with," she responded, in her usual snide tone.

He replied, "I'm not going to hurt her, if that's what you're worried about."

"Someone always gets hurt," Alice retorted, before she darted into the kitchen to put the food on the table.

Brandon turned to look at Mary, and she mouthed the words, *"I'm sorry."* But she wasn't just apologizing for her sister's behavior. She was sorry for her part in everything, too.

The meal went fairly well, considering the tension Alice had caused. Brandon certainly seemed to enjoy the food. He complimented them on their cooking, eating his fair share. He had two helpings of the chicken and dumplings and slathered loads of honey butter on his corn bread.

Afterward, he tried to help with the dishes, but Mary declined his offer, telling him to relax instead. Brandon wandered onto the patio while the women cleaned up. Mary figured he needed a break from Alice. The patio was just a tiny slab of concrete with a café table, but at least it would give him a place to breathe.

Since Brandon was outdoors and out of earshot, Mary waited for Alice to complain about him. And she did, of course, right on cue. "He's so rich and spoiled," she said. "Bringing us expensive gifts and talking about his celebrity dad. It was all I could do not to tell him that you've been playing him, like his dad played our mom."

Mary rinsed the empty potato bowl. "I was scared that you might say something."

"Well, I didn't. But now I'm thinking that you should try to marry this guy and take him for all he's worth."

"What?" Mary lifted her head.

"He's totally falling for you. Any fool can see it. And if you lured him into marrying you, you could get all sorts of expensive things from him. He would go to the ends of the earth to kiss my butt, too, just because I'm your sister."

"I can't believe you're suggesting that." Just the thought of it was making her hands shake.

"So what's the big deal? If you married him, you'd be getting the guy you want."

"I never said I wanted to be his wife."

"But now that I planted the seed, I'll bet you're going to start obsessing about it. Besides, if you married him and let him support us, we'd still be getting justice for Mama. He owes us that much, him and his bastard of a dad. If Kirby had bought Mama's songs like he was supposed to, you wouldn't be working your tail off, and I wouldn't be stuck having to take student loans."

"I would never try to con Brandon into marrying me." To her, that would be the ultimate betrayal, the worst thing she could possibly do. "I need to end it when I can."

"When you can? Seriously, what's stopping you?"

"I'm just not ready."

Alice rolled her eyes. "Why? Because he's such a great lay? I think it's because you're falling in love with him."

"I am not." Mary protested. By now, she was shaking so badly she nearly dropped the plate she was loading into the dishwasher. She couldn't let herself love Brandon. She absolutely, positively couldn't.

After the kitchen was clean, it was time to serve dessert. Mary brought the treats outside to where Brandon was waiting.

He turned and smiled at her, and she nearly melted on the spot. For a woman refusing to fall in love, she was headed for trouble—in the worst kind of way.

Later that evening, Mary went to Brandon's loft with him to spend the night. As they lay in bed, facing each other with moonlight streaming in through the windows, she wondered what it would be like to be his bride.

A shiver traveled down her spine. She had no business imagining herself as his wife. But even as she fought her feelings, she knew that she loved him. God help her, but Alice was right—and it was pointless to pretend otherwise.

He was being quiet, not saying a word. But he was staring at her, as if he had something on his mind. She took a chance and asked, "What are you thinking about?"

"I was just pondering how much I like you."

Her breath rushed out. "You already know how much I like you." They'd discussed it before. But she couldn't tell him that she loved him. She could barely say it to herself. Everything inside her was spinning a mile a minute. But no matter how she felt about him, it would never work. They could never stay together, not for real.

"Alice was pretty much what I expected," he said.

"You were being really nice to her, even when she wasn't very nice to you."

He shrugged. "She has a lot of growing up to do, but she's only nineteen. A lot of people are troubled at that age. She's just a screwed-up kid, looking for attention."

And Mary was a tortured adult who'd gotten herself into a horrible mess. "I should have been a better influence on her."

He frowned. "You can't take responsibility for her actions."

That wasn't true. If she hadn't promised Alice that she would help her get back at Brandon and his dad, none of this would be happening. "In the beginning I tried to teach her right from wrong, but as time went on, I just gave up."

"You're not her parent. You're her sister." He angled his head. "You're being too hard on yourself."

He didn't know the whole story. But she'd blinded him with her nice girl persona. "When we were young and she got upset about something, I didn't stop her from letting it fester. Sometimes I let things fester, too."

He smoothed a strand of hair away from her cheek. "That just makes you human."

A bad human, she thought. Mary still had ill feelings toward Kirby. She still hated him for what he'd done and the domino effect it had on her and Alice.

"I wish you'd confide in me about the rest of your family," Brandon said. "I can tell that something wasn't right with your parents. Things might have been off with your grandma, too."

"Our grandmother was a practical woman, conservative in her beliefs." That much she could tell him. That much she was willing to say. "But she treated us kindly. She was the one who first taught me to bake."

"Whose side of the family was she from?"

"She was our maternal grandmother. She didn't live near us. She only visited now and then." She'd died a few years before Mama. But she'd never known about Kirby. No one in the family had ever told her. Grandma wouldn't have approved of Mama's affair with him. Nor had she been aware of how truly depressed her daughter had been, either. Mama was good at faking it when she had to.

"Alice said something earlier about what a nice lady your mom was." He touched Mary's hair again. "But then she clammed up after she said it."

Her chest went tight. This wasn't a conversation she wanted to have. "It's difficult for us to express our feelings about our mother."

"Did your father hurt her?"

Oh my God. He thought it was *her* dad who'd destroyed Mama. But in reality, it was *his.* She gazed into his eyes, the tightness in her chest working its way to her soul. "I'm sorry, but I just can't talk about this."

"Okay." He blew out a soft sigh. "But if you ever feel the need to talk about it, you can come to me. I'll be here."

"Thank you, but I'd rather keep it to myself."

They both went silent. Far too silent, she thought. She felt as if the room was going to crash in on her, right along with her heart.

A few painful seconds later, she said, "I didn't want you to buy me the fairy painting, but now I'm glad that you did." When their affair was over, it would be something warm and soft and magical to remember him by.

"That picture is meant for you."

"It definitely is." But loving him wasn't a cure for her deception. It wasn't lessening the shame or the guilt. If anything, it magnified it.

He lowered the strap on her nightgown. She'd worn a baby doll nightie to bed. Something far too innocent for the person she'd become. Far too sweet. Mary closed her eyes. She felt like such a fraud.

"What do you have on under this cute little thing?" he asked.

She opened her eyes. "Matching panties." She'd bought the ensemble to entice him. But now she wondered what she'd been trying to prove by resorting to girlish lingerie.

"Mmm." He reached down and slipped his hand into her panties. "It suits you."

No, it didn't, she thought. But he was making her wet just the same. She rocked her hips, rubbing against his seductive touch. He was already naked; that was how he slept every night.

They kissed, and the foreplay continued. She went

after him, stroking him between his legs, giving him pleasure, too.

Soon he was peeling off her panties and tossing them onto the side of the bed. He did away with her nightie, as well.

He removed a condom from the drawer next to him and said, "You can put this on me tonight. There's no hurry. You can take your time. We can both enjoy it."

As familiar as she'd become with his body, this was just another layer of excitement. She opened the packet, and he guided her through it. She loved touching him.

Once he was sheathed, he braced himself above her. She opened her legs, inviting him inside.

He thrust deep, and they made long, warm, luxurious love, with breathless whispers between them.

Mary awakened in the middle of the night. No matter how hard she tried, she wasn't able to go back to sleep. So she finally crept out of bed and got dressed in the bathroom, careful not to disturb Brandon.

After leaving him a note, in case he woke up and noticed she was gone, she went to a twenty-four-hour market and bought the ingredients she needed to bake a special batch of cupcakes. Thanks to Brandon's chef, his kitchen was stocked with the cookware, utensils and appliances she required.

Hours later, while she was putting the finishing touches on the cupcakes, Brandon entered the kitchen. He was wrapped in a robe and handsomely tousled from sleep. She wasn't surprised to see him this early. It was Sunday, and he would be taking Cline to the park. For now, she assumed the dog was still crashed out in his own room.

"What are you doing, pretty lady?" Brandon asked.

"Making goodies for Tommy and Sophie." She showed him her handiwork. The pink cupcakes were artfully decorated with Zoe's name on them.

He studied them. "Oh, those are cute."

"I also made banana nut bread for you." She gestured to where it was cooling on a counter.

"Wow. I slept through all of this?" He cut a piece of the bread and munched on it. "As always, your treats are amazing." He brewed a pot of coffee while she packed up the cupcakes.

"Will you take these to Tommy and Sophie the next time you see them?" she asked. "If it's not within the next day or so, I can freeze them, and you can bring them whenever it's convenient for you."

"I can pay them a quick visit today. But you should come with me. You should give them the cupcakes yourself. We can go after we take Cline for his walk."

"Oh, I'm sorry. But I promised a coworker that I would work for her today. It's just for a few hours this afternoon, but I'll need to go home soon."

He poured the coffee and handed her a cup. He added cream to his, and she used sugar.

"I'm going to miss you," he said.

"I'll miss you, too." She looked into his eyes, battling her heart, struggling to cope with her feelings. Yesterday Alice had asked her why she was taking so long to end things with Brandon. And now Mary had no recourse but to ask herself the same question. How long was she going to keep this affair going? How long was she going to cling to him, falling deeper and deeper in love? "Do you still want me to go to Matt's wedding with you?" she asked.

He glanced up, gazing at her over the rim of his cup.

"Of course I do." He put the coffee down. "Does this mean you decided you're going to take the trip with me? Or are you still just batting the idea around?"

"I'm still batting it around." But at this point, maybe it would behoove her to attend a Talbot family function. To come face-to-face with Kirby. To meet the man who'd destroyed her mother, and remind herself once and for all why she couldn't keep seeing Brandon.

She ached inside, just thinking about it. But it would give her a timeline, a schedule to follow. Otherwise, she might never summon the courage to end the relationship.

"You know what?" she said. "I think I should go with you." She moved closer to him. "But I don't know what's going to happen afterward."

The muscles in his face tightened. "What's that supposed to mean? That you're going to stop seeing me after the wedding?"

"We both know that we can't stay together forever.

Sooner or later we'll have to go back to our regular lives." She tried to sound rational, to force herself to seem strong. Yet all she really wanted to do was cry. "No matter how hard we try, we're never going to fit into each other's worlds."

He quickly argued, "I'm completely willing to bring you into mine."

"By me wearing ball gowns and learning to waltz? It's not that simple, Brandon. I can't be around socialites who are going to look down their noses at me. I don't want them misinterpreting my feelings for you or calling me a gold digger." Even Alice had tried to get Mary to lure him into marriage for his money. "It's just not feasible." At least this way she could pretend that their affair had been based on something pure, instead of deception and lies.

"I don't care what other people think. Besides, I already told you that my friends have been encouraging me to find a nice girl." He pulled her into his arms. "When we get back from Texas, we're going to figure this out."

"There's nothing to figure out." She already loved him; she was already doomed. "I'm not the right woman for you."

"You're exasperating, that's what you are." He held her tighter. "And I'll be damned if I'm going to let you break it off before I'm ready."

"So when are you going to be ready?" How long was it going to be before he stopped wanting her? Before he didn't care anymore and moved on?

"Hell if I know." His voice went ragged. "I've never needed anyone the way I need you."

Mary squeezed her eyes shut. Had he fallen for her as deeply as she'd fallen for him? Alice certainly seemed to think so. "It's all so confusing."

"Tell me about it." He tugged on her braid, nudging her head back and kissing her hard and quick.

Her knees turned to jelly. If there was one thing Brandon knew how to do, it was to seduce her. After he lifted his mouth from hers, she said, "You make me weak."

"And you make me frustrated. You're the most challenging woman I've ever been with. And you're so damned mysterious, too. Nothing about you comes easy."

She could scarcely breathe. "Except for when you make me come."

He smiled a wicked smile. "There is that. The sex has definitely been good."

Too good, she thought, as he hauled her into the bedroom and stripped her bare. Not just her body, but her heart and her soul, too. Mary was never, ever going to be the same, not after falling in love with a man she couldn't keep.

Ten

Brandon took Cline to the park, then brought the cupcakes to Tommy's house. His brother seemed impressed with Mary's work.

He even took some pictures for his Instagram page to show them off. He was particularly pleased that they had Zoe's name on them. By now, he and Sophie had introduced their daughter to the world, by way of social media and the press.

"Mary agreed to attend Matt's wedding with me," Brandon said, as he and his brother sat outside in the sunshine, occupying a bench in front of an enormous jeweled tiger statue Tommy had bought for his garden. Sophie and the baby were inside, napping.

"That's good news." Tommy sipped from a recyclable water bottle.

"Yes, it is. But not completely. She's talking about ending it after we get back from Texas. She's always saying things like that. She's never been secure about dating me."

"I'm sorry she keeps pulling away from you. But I can see where she feels insecure. She's just a regular girl, and you're a big society guy from a celebrity family."

"That's the reason she keeps giving." Brandon heaved a sigh. "But I still think there's more to her story."

"The last time we talked, you mentioned her family and that you thought that her dad might have been hurtful or abusive to her mom. Do you still think that's what happened?"

"I don't know. I questioned her about it, but she said that she didn't want to discuss it." Yet the more she remained silent, the more concerned Brandon became. "I think that whatever occurred with her parents is affecting her relationship with me. I think that's the main issue." Sometimes when he looked into Mary's eyes, he saw how fragile she was. Like this morning, he thought. She'd seemed especially vulnerable.

Tommy swigged his water. "How'd the dinner go with her sister?"

"It was weird, but Mary warned me that Alice wasn't going to like me. She liked the artwork I gave her, though. She definitely seems like a materialistic girl. Mary isn't that way. Possessions aren't important to her." But he was glad that she'd accepted the fairy painting from him.

"You brought the sister a gift?"

"It seemed like the thing to do."

Tommy laughed a little. "You better be careful or you'll turn into Dad."

"That's not funny." Ever since Kirby got clean and sober and was trying to become a better father, he'd been showering them and Matt with overly sentimental presents. Mostly to make up for the years he'd spent on the road. They'd barely seen him when they were growing up, and Matt had seen him even less. "Speaking of gifts, I shopped online before I came over here today and ordered a big stuffed husky dog for Zoe. But it's not from me, it's from Cline."

His brother smiled. "Is it a girl husky with a pink bow?"

"Yep." Brandon smiled, too. "I showed Cline its picture, and he gave me his approval."

"Yeah. I'm sure he did." Tommy shifted on the bench. "You're already turning into an incredible uncle. I think you'll make a great dad someday, too, if you ever decide to have kids."

Brandon's thoughts turned to his lover, to the woman driving him mad. "I just wish I wasn't so consumed with Mary." He frowned, troubled by her effect on him. "Maybe I should just let her break it off after the wedding and be done with it."

"That's totally up to you, bro. But you already seem miserable about losing her."

"I don't know how to reason with her." He'd never

been so flustered by anyone. "She just keeps stating the same case, insisting that we don't belong together. But if I knew where her head was really at, if I knew what the deal with her parents was, maybe I could understand her better."

"You could do a security check and look into her past. You've got lots of resources for that."

"Yes, but in a situation like this, poking around in her family history seems pretty damn invasive." He'd never investigated anyone he'd ever dated. Of course, he'd never dated anyone as secretive as Mary. Still, could he take his curiosity that far? "It's not as if she's posing a security threat."

Tommy shrugged. "It was just a thought."

"I need to give myself some time to think about it."

"If things are still rocky with her after the wedding, maybe you could look into it then."

"I guess we'll see." The Texas trip was still three weeks away. "I'd rather not do it if I don't have to. But it's been tough trying to figure her out."

"I knew Sophie all my life, better than anyone. Of course we went through a rough patch when we were falling in love. Those are some scary feelings at first. But you know how tough it was for me. You and Matt helped me through it."

That was true; they had. But that didn't make Brandon an expert. He didn't want to think about how frightening it would be to fall in love with Mary. He had his hands full with how badly he needed her. Loving her would only make it harder.

Tommy's phone dinged, signaling a text. "Dad is here."

Brandon struggled to focus. "What?"

"Dad just stopped by to see the baby. But she's still asleep, so Dottie is sending him out here to hang out with us."

In no time, they spotted Kirby cutting across the lawn. As always, he looked like an outlaw, decked in black.

"Hey, boys," he said, by way of a greeting.

They both responded, and he sat on the base of the tiger statue, placing himself across from them. Kirby's graying beard was neatly trimmed and his eyes were deep and dark beneath a straw Stetson.

Brandon considered his father's past and the women in it. His former mistresses, including Matt's mom, had been regular girls, not starlets or groupies. Brandon and Tommy's mother was the most glamorous woman Dad had ever been with, but she still had the gentle nature he was drawn to. Mom had certainly deserved a better husband, but at least they were friends now.

"Are you seeing anyone yet?" Brandon asked him, curious if he'd followed through on his plans to start dating again.

"No. But I put the word out there with friends. No one seems to want to set me up with anyone, though."

"You don't exactly have the best track record," Tommy interjected. "So they're probably just being cautious."

Kirby nodded. "I might have to use a professional

matchmaker. Or a dating site for rich old farts." He chuckled. "There's got to be an app for that, right?"

Tommy chuckled, too. "If there isn't, then we should create one just for you."

Brandon smiled, going along with their goofy joke. But overall, he couldn't stop thinking about Mary. He went ahead and told his dad, "I'm dating someone special. I don't know how long it's going to last, but she's a sweet girl."

"If she's that sweet, you ought to try to keep her."

"I'm working on it." Or he was trying to, anyway. "She'll be coming to Matt's wedding with me. So you'll get to meet her then."

"Sounds like a plan." Kirby arched his back. "So when did you start seeing nice girls? Weren't the diva types more your style?"

"She inspired me to change my pattern." She was inspiring him to feel more than he might be able to handle, too.

Like the possibility of falling in love, he thought. And the big, shaky fear that went with it.

As the weeks passed, the wedding crept nearer and nearer. And finally, the time arrived. In fact, Mary would be boarding a private plane this very day, en route to Texas. At this point, she was in so deep she couldn't escape if she tried.

Every moment she spent with Brandon was more powerful than the last. She was starting to feel as if she'd known him her entire life. But she doubted that he could say the same thing about her. Was she going to end the relationship when their trip was over? Would meeting Kirby give her the strength to do it? Or would she keep putting off the inevitable?

When she finished packing, she brought her luggage into the entryway and set it beside the front door. Brandon was sending a limo to pick her up. He had some loose ends to tie up in his office this morning, so he would be meeting her at the airport.

Mary glanced into the living room, where Alice brooded on the couch. Her sister turned and said, "Well, look at you, preparing to go to Texas and make friends with Kirby."

She blew out a sigh. "I'm not going to become friends with him. I still hate him as much as you do."

"What if you stop hating him? What if he cons you into trusting him like he did with Mama, and you fall into the Talbot trap?"

Mary was already falling into it with Brandon, but he wasn't phony like his dad. He was the real deal. "I'm not going to let Kirby con me."

Tears rushed to her sister's eyes, but she quickly wiped them away. She looked oddly innocent today, with a pair of fuzzy skull-and-crossbones slippers on her feet.

"It was all a mistake," Alice said.

Mary sat beside her on the sofa. "What was?"

"The stupid revenge plot I came up with. I should have known better than to expect you to follow through on it the way it was intended."

"Please stop blaming me for caring about Brandon. I can't help it if I developed feelings for him.

Besides, do you know how painful it is for me to be deceiving him? To look into his eyes and pretend to be someone I'm not? This hasn't been a picnic for me, and now I have to figure out when and how to end it without hurting him more than I already have."

"I still think you should try to charm him into marrying you. At least then we'd be getting something out of this. But instead, you're going to walk away with nothing. And leave me with nothing."

"I can't make this about money." Mary couldn't do that to Brandon. "And how long do you think we'd be able to stand being related to Kirby? Just think of what a nightmare that would be."

"I wouldn't care if it made us rich, and I don't think Mama would've cared, either. You know how badly she wanted to give us a better life."

Mary shook her head. "Yes, she wanted good things for us. But I doubt she would've approved of me marrying Brandon and using him as a sugar daddy." She studied Alice's expression. Her baby sister was pouting something awful. "That isn't who I am."

"I know you love him. And don't deny it this time. I can tell you do."

"You're right. I am in love with him. And that's exactly why I have to break it off."

"And you're hoping that meeting Kirby will motivate you to let Brandon go? That your disdain for his dad will be the catalyst that frees you? Well, good luck with that, Miss Goody Two Shoes."

"Don't poke fun at me. I'm just trying to do what I think is right for Brandon."

"But not what's right for me?" Alice got up and stormed into her room, slamming the door behind her.

Mary heaved a sigh. Between deceiving Brandon and fighting with her sister, things were a mess. But instead of chasing after Alice, she let her stew. She loved her sister, but she couldn't keep coddling her. It might do Alice some good to be left alone. For now, Mary had her own problems.

She checked the time. The limo would be here soon, and later today she would be in the Texas Hill Country, surrounded by Brandon and his family.

The Flying Creek Ranch was a remarkable place, steeped in nature. Mary and Brandon's cabin presented a spectacular view of the hills, and the decor was rife with Western memorabilia and Indian artifacts.

Mary hadn't met Matt or Libby yet. One of Matt's employees had gotten her and Brandon settled into their cabin. Of course, the bride and groom weren't causing her distress. She wasn't worried about making their acquaintance. It was Kirby who consumed her.

The rehearsal dinner was tonight, and she and Brandon were getting ready to go. This was it, she thought, the moment where she would come face-to-face with his father. She was so nervous, she felt as if her heart was sinking in her chest.

"You look pretty," Brandon said to her.

"Thank you." She was attired in a yellow eyelet dress and tan cowboy boots. She'd bought several Western-style outfits for the trip, using money from the overtime she'd put in at work. If Alice hadn't been so mad at her over the past few weeks, she would have engaged her help. But as it was, Mary had chosen her clothes on her own. "You look handsome, too."

"Wait until you see me in my tux tomorrow. This is the second wedding I've been part of this year. First it was Tommy's, and now this one."

"Always the groomsman and never the groom?" Without thinking about how it sounded, she teased him, regretting the words right after they passed her lips.

"I was Tommy's best man, but that premise still works, I guess." He came to stand beside her in the mirror. "Maybe I'll get married someday. Maybe I'll see it as something I'm capable of doing."

The sinking feeling in her heart turned darker, lonelier. "I think you'd make a great husband someday." For someone else, she thought. Not for her.

He turned toward her. "I know I shouldn't be starting a conversation like this when we're so close to heading out the door. But I have feelings for you that scare me. You've really done a number on me, Mary."

She'd done a number on both of them. "What I feel for you scares me, too."

"You've been uncertain around me ever since the

day we met." He touched a strand of her unbound hair. "But I'm glad you came on this trip with me. I'm happy you're here."

He didn't look happy. He looked like a man who was on the verge of falling in love. Did he know that was why he was scared? Or hadn't he realized it yet? She certainly knew that she loved him, for whatever that was worth.

"We better go before we're late." She still had to deal with the anguish of meeting his father.

"Yeah, we'd better." He stepped back. "But after we come back here tonight, I'm going to put my hands all over you."

"I'd be disappointed if you didn't." She wanted to make love with him, as many times as she could.

Before it all came to an end.

The rehearsal dinner was in the dining room at the lodge, with knotty pine walls, limestone floors and big, bright chandeliers. Mary sat with the Talbots at their linen-draped table. Somehow, Kirby ended up next to her, with Brandon on her other side. Was the seating arrangement a joke from the universe? A punishment? She'd expected to meet Kirby, but she hadn't expected to be sandwiched between him and Brandon.

Mary could barely eat. She picked at her pasta, moving it around on her plate.

No doubt about it, Kirby was a charming man. He smiled; he made lighthearted jokes; he spoke with pride about his children and raved about his new granddaughter. He also bragged about Chance and how the boy had been named after one of his songs.

As overwhelming as this was, she could see where her mother had found him appealing. There was no denying his star power. Every time he looked at Mary, his eyes sparkled. He even patted her hand a few times. Clearly, he sensed her shyness and was trying to make her comfortable. He was being ridiculously nice. Painfully nice. And it made her want to scream, to yell, to shout at him, to defend her mother. But she kept quiet, the lump in her throat getting bigger with each breath she took.

Brandon's mother was kind and friendly, too. And beautiful. Mary had never seen a more gorgeous woman, with her long lean figure and silky blond hair. Everyone was treating Mary with care, doing their best to help her fit in. She'd already met Tommy and Sophie, so being around them helped a little.

But still, no one knew why she was so nervous. No one knew the truth. When people began to mingle, visiting guests at other tables, Brandon was called away for a quick meeting with the other groomsmen. He promised that he would be right back.

For Mary, being alone with his father was torture. The worst thing she could've imagined.

He leaned over and said to her, "My son is really smitten with you. You're the first woman I've ever seen him care so much about."

"I care about him, too." Her voice quavered. "Brandon is a good person."

"He's a lot better than I am. My family has put up with a lot of terrible things from me."

"I read something about that in your biography." It was the only response she could think to say.

"Well, then you know of what I speak." He sipped his ginger ale. "I'm lucky that Matt allowed me back into his life, let alone let me be part of his wedding."

Mary glanced at the groom, who stood at the bar, chatting with the bride's family. Tomorrow Matt would be exchanging vows with the love of his life. "He and Libby make a beautiful couple." She'd seen how tenderly they'd interacted with each other over dinner. "Libby is a doll." A bright and shimmering girl, Mary thought, who seemed as happy and content as a bride should be.

Kirby nodded. "Yes, she most certainly is. Without Libby, I don't think Matt would have ever forgiven me. She influenced him to make amends with me."

If Mary stayed with Brandon could they influence each other to make things right? Could he forgive her for deceiving him, and could she stop hating Kirby for what he'd done to her mother?

With that thought spiraling in her head, she stared at Brandon's father. Could she make things work with Brandon or was she dreaming of a fantasy that could never be?

"You seem sort of familiar," Kirby said suddenly.

Her heart nearly blasted its way out of her chest. "I don't know what you mean." Did he sense a likeness between her and her mother? That would seem odd. Mary didn't resemble Mama.

"It's just something about you. Maybe it's your girl-next-door quality. Matt's mother was like that when I met her." He gestured to his former mistress, a lovely fiftysomething brunette who sat at another table with her husband. "I made a mess out of her life, keeping her on the string the way I did. But she's happy now with someone else."

Mary relaxed a little. He was comparing her to Matt's mother, not her own. Then again, he'd branded Mama a stalker, so likening Mary to her wouldn't make much sense.

Kirby smiled at her. "You're easy to talk to. But that's obvious, I guess, with me doing most of the talking."

"I don't mind." It was easier for her to stay quiet.

"I hope you and Brandon can make a go of things. It would be nice to keep seeing you at other family gatherings."

"Thank you," she replied, fretful about surviving this gathering, let alone more of them. She was actually starting to like Kirby, to view him as something other than a monster.

She could only imagine how upset Alice would be if she knew that Mary was bonding with Brandon's father.

She said, "You seem nicer than I assumed you'd be."

"Because of my arrogant reputation? As much as I hate to say it, I still have my pompous-ass moments."

He lowered his voice. "But I'm genuinely sorry for the pain I caused the people in my life."

Would he admit fault for what he'd done to Mama? Would he take responsibility for it? Would he say he was sorry? Or would he insist that she was the stalker he'd made her out to be?

Mary was so confused she could barely see straight. Brandon returned to the table and leaned in to kiss her on the cheek. She loved him so much she ached from it.

Kirby said to his son, "I like your lady. She's sweet."

"I told you that she was," Brandon replied with a smile.

His father smiled, too, and got up to excuse himself. "I think I'll go hunt down my new grandbaby. As far as I know, the nanny hasn't put her to bed yet. Have you seen how excited Chance is about her? They're going to make great cousins." He tipped his hat to Mary. "You be good to my boy, okay?"

"I will," she said, even if that ship had sailed. How could she promise to be good to Brandon when she was lying about who she was?

He kissed her again, this time on the lips, and she closed her eyes, lost in the sensation of him.

Later that night, Mary and Brandon made love with vigor and passion. She couldn't get enough of him, and he couldn't seem to get enough of her, either. His hands were everywhere, touching, caressing, playing across her body and creating powerful ripples. Like waves, she thought. Like the sea at midnight, rising up in a storm.

Their mouths came together, tongues mating, teeth clashing. He growled in her ear, and she used her nails like weapons, digging into his skin.

She turned toward the window, where a three-quarter moon shone through the trees, casting a shadowy glow on their cabin.

She loved being here with him, deep in the Texas Hill Country. Even as painful as it was to be around his family, she felt as if she belonged with Brandon.

It was a false sense of belonging, she reminded herself.

They rolled across the bed, twisting the top sheet and knocking soft, fluffy pillows onto the rugged hardwood floor. Their clothes were strewn on the floor, too, just where they'd left them. She could see her bra and panties, her dress, her boots, one of which had fallen on its side, its heel upended. Her heart was falling, too, spiraling down a rabbit hole and spinning out of control.

As her thoughts scattered, Brandon pushed deeper, moving inside her like a madman.

Soon, they switched positions so she could straddle him. She bounced up and down, holding on to his shoulders for support.

But she couldn't steady her feelings. She couldn't stop loving him. It was too late for that.

He watched her with a hot gleam in his eyes, hungry for her to take him all the way, to make him come.

She leaned forward to kiss him, but it was a bit-ing kiss, rife with sexual chaos and friction. When she removed her mouth from his, she increased the tempo, giving them both the orgasm that they wanted, needed, had to have.

They climaxed together—all the way.

In the seconds that followed, she collapsed on top of him, and he skimmed a gentle hand down her spine.

"It just gets better and better with you," he said.

He meant the sex, obviously. She caught her breath and replied, "You're all I want. You're all I think about."

"Likewise." He met her gaze. "Shower with me?"

It was an invitation she couldn't refuse. She wanted to get wet and soapy with him. "Definitely."

They went into the bathroom, and he disposed of the condom. The tub doubled as a shower, but it was smaller than the other shower stalls they'd used at Brandon's homes. Mary didn't mind. She liked being ridiculously close to him.

They washed the sex off their bodies, but it didn't leave their thoughts. They were still looking at each other with satisfaction in their eyes.

Afterward, they dried off and returned to bed, naked and clean. By now, they'd righted the bed, smoothing the sheets and replacing the pillows they'd knocked onto the floor.

As they lay side by side, gazing up at the ceiling, he said, "You made a wonderful impression on my family. They all really like you."

She did her best to seem calm, even if her pulse had begun to skitter. "I like them, too."

"Even my dad?"

The skittering continued. "Yes. He was very kind and complimentary to me."

"So the stuff that was in his book doesn't bother you anymore?"

"No." But what he'd done to her mother still did. She turned to face Brandon. She couldn't stand lying to him anymore. God help her, but she was going to tell him the truth, every last painful detail. Only now wasn't the time to do it. She would wait until the wedding was over and they were back in Nashville. She would tell him that she loved him then, too. She would spill all her secrets.

She had no idea where the truth would lead. But at least her conscience would be clear. And maybe, just maybe, they could make their relationship work.

He skimmed her cheek with his fingers. "You never cease to baffle me, Mary. You and your mysterious ways."

The confusion would be over soon, she thought. Once she told him the truth, he would know everything about her.

As ashamed as she was about what she'd done to Brandon, she hoped and prayed that he would consider the pain his dad had cast upon her family. That alone should absolve her.

Shouldn't it?

Needing to hide her expression, to shield her emotions, she moved into his arms and buried her face against his shoulder.

He touched her still-damp hair and asked, "What's wrong?"

"Nothing." Her response was muffled against his skin. "I just want to be close to you."

"Are you certain that's all it is?"

"Yes." She had no choice but to lie. Her final lie, she thought, the last of the tall tales.

"That's okay. I don't mind keeping you close." He nuzzled the top of her head with his chin. "I'll hold you until you fall asleep."

"Thank you." Although sleep would probably elude her, she closed her eyes, letting Brandon be her hero. Her dream lover, she thought, wrapped up in the stars and the moon and the secrets that still shrouded them.

Eleven

The wedding was sweetly romantic, Brandon thought. Beautiful in a way that he'd never experienced before. Matt and Libby had a history with National S'mores Day, and that's the day they'd chosen to get married.

The happy couple exchanged vows at dusk, surrounded by trees and hills and people they loved. Libby made a stunning bride, draped in a long shimmery dress, her white-blond hair adorned with flowers. Matt stood tall and strong, attired in a black tuxedo and Western hat.

Security was tight. There was no press on the premises. The family had done an excellent job of keeping it private.

As Brandon watched the ceremony, he glanced

over at Mary. She seemed mesmerized by it all. She still baffled him, of course. Nothing had changed in that regard. He still considered his lover a mystery. But now he was wondering how it would be to spend the rest of his life with her, to fall madly in love, to get married.

Maybe he was already in love with her. If he wasn't, he wouldn't be having those sorts of thoughts. But it wasn't a calm feeling. He was even more scared of his feelings for her than he'd been before.

Suddenly Brandon was anxious for Matt and Libby's vows to end and for the reception to begin. He needed to escape this setting and have a quick, stiff drink.

Finally, Brandon got his wish. The reception offered an open bar. He ordered his whiskey neat and downed the amber liquid in a few anxious gulps. Normally Brandon was more controlled. In fact, he never resorted to alcohol to relax his nerves. That just wasn't his style. But it wasn't every day a man found himself falling in love with a woman he barely knew.

He considered a second drink, but decided against it. He would be better off trying to keep a clear head, to remain true to his normally controlled nature.

"Are you okay?" Mary asked him, as she sipped champagne. "You seem distracted."

"I'm fine," he replied. "I'm hungry, though. Are you?"

"Yes." She smiled at him.

But even in the midst of her smile, he noticed a haunted look in her eyes. Was she still thinking of leaving him? When they returned from Texas, would she disappear into a soft gray mist?

They headed for the buffet, where a feast of down-home cooking and uptown delicacies made a marvelous presentation.

Brandon and Mary filled their plates and socialized with other guests. As the celebration continued, the house band played cover tunes. Dad and Tommy sat in with them for a number of songs, making it a star-studded event. Needless to say, the music was spectacular.

"At least I don't have to worry about not knowing how to waltz tonight," Mary said.

Brandon nodded. It was country dancing, through and through. "Do you want to take a spin?"

"Yes, please." Her gaze met his. "It'll be our first time dancing together."

He reached for her hand. "Yes, indeed." There were lots of firsts zipping through his mind: the first day they'd met, their first date, their first kiss. She'd bewitched him from the beginning, and she was still doing it.

The music was fast and fun. Brandon had grown up on country songs. He knew them inside out.

He spun Mary around, and she two-stepped with the best of them. She was wearing the same boots she'd worn to last night's rehearsal dinner, only now they were getting some miles on them.

After a while, the band switched gears, slowing the music down. They played a variety of emotional ballads, packed with romance.

Brandon held Mary close, and they swayed rhythmically to the dreamy riffs. He couldn't deny how compatible they were, locked in each other's arms. Their bodies just seemed to fit, motion to motion, breath to breath, similar to when they made love.

"It's nice that we're going to have two more days here," she said. "I've never imagined being on a vacation like this before."

He'd been on lots of holidays, all over the world. But this was the most compelling—the scariest, too, with how deep and shaky his notion about loving her was.

She nestled closer to him. "I'm excited about going horseback riding tomorrow. And hiking and fishing the day after that."

He was glad that she was having a good time. But it was almost as if she was trying too hard to make this trip memorable. He even got the feeling that she was trying to convince herself that everything was going to be all right.

Whatever "everything" was, he thought. Mary's past wasn't any clearer today than it had been two months ago. And Brandon didn't know if he could take much more of being left in the dark.

He wanted answers. He wanted to know exactly who Mary McKenzie was and why she refused to talk about her parents. No matter how hard he tried, he couldn't make heads or tails of her life. He could look forever and still not see past the clouds in her eyes.

After they stopped dancing, they separated, with

Mary wandering over to the bar to try the s'mores martinis that were being handed out.

Brandon took the opportunity to approach Tommy, who was also alone for now.

He said to his brother, "I'm going to do it."

"Do what?" Tommy asked.

"Run a security check on Mary and find out more about her. I'll email them tonight so they can get started on it. Then hopefully, by the time we get back to Nashville, I'll have some answers."

"Maybe her past won't be as traumatic as you think it's going to be."

"There's no point in speculating until I get the report." But at least he was going to find out for himself. At least he would have some clarity amid the chaos of falling in love.

Brandon spent the next few days with Mary, engaging in ranch activities. But the security check he'd requested was never far from his mind.

Then, on the day they arrived back in Nashville, he got word that the report was ready.

He was still with Mary, dropping her off at her apartment, when the call came. Once he parked in front of her place, they sat in the car, saying their goodbyes.

"I'm sorry I can't take you home with me," he said. "I have to go to my office today."

"It's okay. I need to unpack and get settled back in. I need to see Alice, too. I haven't spoken to my sister since I've been gone. We got in a fight right before I left."

He didn't ask what the tiff had been about. He was already aware of how moody her sister was. "Then you need to patch things up."

"Yes, I do." She smiled softly at him. "I had a wonderful time in Texas with you."

"It did turn out nice." But that didn't stop him from stressing about the choice he'd made to investigate her. If she knew what he was up to, would she be hurt or angry? Would she feel betrayed by him?

"Is there something going on at your work?" she asked suddenly.

He frowned. "What?"

"You seem anxious about going to the office."

He answered the best he could. "There's a report I need to tend to." He frowned again. "I could have received it as an email, but I had them drop off a hard copy to my assistant instead. I didn't want this information in an electronic file." He wanted it waiting on his desk in a sealed envelope, where he could brace himself before he paged through it.

"Is it something bad?"

As evasive as Mary was about her past, he didn't see how the report was going to contain something good. It was obvious that her problems stemmed from her parents, but to what extent, he couldn't say. "I just need to read it."

"Then you better go do that," she said.

"Yeah, I guess I better." He cupped her chin in both hands. As guilty as he felt for investigating her, he was still doing it for the right reasons. He needed to know who she was and what made her tick. He needed to come to terms with loving her, too. For now, it was like loving a stranger. "I'll call you later, okay?"

"Okay." She leaned forward, and they kissed.

Her lips tasted fresh and minty beneath his. So soft, so enticing, so confusing.

He ended the kiss, overwhelmed with the knowledge that he loved her. But as soon as he got his hands on the report, the puzzle that was Mary would be solved. He was overwhelmed by that, too. He wanted to help her get past her pain and whatever had caused it. But was he capable of restoring the damage, of making it better?

"Let me help you with your luggage," he said, and popped the trunk.

They exited the car, and he lifted her bag and wheeled it to her door. They kissed one more time, on the stoop, holding each other unbearably close.

He released her, wishing that she'd been comfortable confiding in him. It would've been so much easier than having her investigated.

She tried the door, but it was locked. "I guess Alice isn't home. School started this week, so she might have a class today." Mary removed her keys from her purse.

He stood back and watched her go inside. She glanced back and waved, and that was it. Their vacation together was officially over.

He returned to his BMW and zoomed off to his

office. Traffic was heavy, making his drive longer than usual.

Finally, he arrived. He entered the building and went straight to his desk. He opened the envelope and settled into his chair to read.

Within minutes, his chest twisted in pain, as if someone had stuck a knife clean through it.

The woman he loved was a liar, a con, an emotional cheat. According to the document in his hand, she was the daughter of Catherine Lynn Birch, a woman he and his father had filed a restraining order against eight years prior. Hell and damnation. Her mom had harassed his dad.

He kept reading, getting the rest of Mary's history. Her parents had lived together but were never married and never owned a home. Her father, Joel David McKenzie, was a truck driver who'd died when Mary was seven and Alice was just a month shy of her first birthday. He was self-employed and didn't have life insurance. The family moved to a smaller rental after he was gone and struggled even more to make ends meet.

There was no domestic abuse that came up. Her dad wasn't the villain in this story. It was her mother who couldn't be trusted. Catherine, or Cathy as she preferred to be called, had died earlier this year, leaving two grieving daughters behind. Two young women, he thought, who were obviously plotting against his family. Why else would Mary have just happened to show up at the park on the day they'd met?

Brandon considered her motives. Was it money?

Was she more materialistic than she'd led him to believe? Was that the end game? Or was it something more sinister?

He read further. Some of what Mary had told him about her past was true. Alice was a party girl who had lots of boyfriends, and Mary was a proper young woman who'd kept her nose to the grindstone and dated her coworker at the bakery in Oklahoma where she'd worked. But that wasn't enough to make Brandon trust her. With the way she'd lured him into loving her, she was far more dangerous than her wild little sister.

In the wake of finishing the report, he wanted to scream at himself for being stupid. He'd brought Mary to Tommy's mansion to see the baby. He'd taken her to Matt's wedding. He'd welcomed her into his family, giving her carte blanche in their carefully protected lives. He'd even allowed her access to his home, anytime she wanted it.

He picked up his phone and called security at his loft, instructing them to change the code and keys. He never should've given them to Mary to begin with.

Brandon shook his head. He'd stepped out of his social circle and look what happened. He'd gotten swindled by the daughter of one of his dad's old stalkers.

Never again, he thought. No more supposedly innocent women. He was so raging mad, so hurt, so frustrated, he wanted to take legal action. But at this point, Mary hadn't actually committed a crime. The judgment had been against her mother, not her. And since Cathy had never violated the terms of the restraining order, she'd more or less been forgotten.

Nonetheless, he was going to confront Mary in a big way. But he wasn't going to return to her apartment. A public place wouldn't do, either. He didn't need any distractions. He decided he would do it here, in the privacy of his office. He didn't want her to suspect that she was under scrutiny, though. He intended to blindside her, just as she'd done to him.

Mary received a text from Brandon, asking her if she would come to his office around two. He said that he had a surprise for her.

She couldn't imagine why he wanted to see her so soon after dropping her off at her apartment, or what his surprise entailed, but she was excited about seeing him again. He'd even included little hearts and flowers emoticons in his message, leading her to believe this was going to be a romantic encounter.

Had he lied about rushing off to read a report? Had he dashed over to his office to set up her surprise?

Since Alice wasn't home yet, Mary had the bathroom to herself. She freshened up, adding a bit more lipstick and fluffing her hair. She was still wearing her traveling clothes. But if things got sexy with Brandon, he would probably divest her of them, anyway.

A niggle of fear and guilt crept in. Now that their trip was over, she'd promised herself that she would tell him the truth. But she couldn't do it today, not in the middle of his surprise.

She took a deep breath and left the house. A short time later, she arrived at his office, which was located in a charming old building near the Country Music Hall of Fame Museum. His suite was on the top floor.

His assistant, a young man with a beard and a trendy haircut, greeted her in the lobby. She hadn't expected anyone else to be there except Brandon.

The assistant called Brandon and let him know that his two o' clock appointment had arrived. Butterflies rushed to her stomach. It all seemed so formal.

"Mr. Talbot will see you now," the assistant said, gesturing down the hallway. "His office is the second door on the left. You don't need to knock. You can go right in."

"Thank you." She made her way to the designated door and opened it.

Brandon sat at his shiny black desk, with a colorful view of downtown Nashville behind him. He wasn't looking particularly romantic. In fact, he looked cool and detached.

Something was wrong. Very, very wrong.

"Close the door and have a seat," he said.

She did as he asked, shutting them in together, then perched on the edge of a leather chair that was positioned across from his desk.

"How does it feel to be brought here under false

pretenses?" he asked, his blue eyes narrowing in on hers.

The hearts and flowers in his text had been a ruse, she realized. But even more disturbing was the folder that was sitting on his desk with her name typed across the front of it.

He pushed it toward her, but she didn't open it. She didn't need to know what it said. She already knew. He'd uncovered her identity.

"I'm sorry," she said, wishing she could go back in time and erase everything she'd done. "I was going to tell you everything. Honestly, I was."

"Really? How convenient for you now that you got caught." He leaned back in his chair, with a dark and lawyerly air. "Do you know why I had you investigated? Because I cared about you and wanted to help you get past whatever was going on in your life. Hell, I was even fancying myself in love with you."

She nearly pitched forward. Now the room felt as it were spinning. She'd begun to assume that he loved her, but she'd never expected to hear it like this. "I fell in love with you, too."

"And I'm supposed to believe that? You've been conning me from the start. Admit it, Mary. This was a scam from day one."

"I do love you. I swear I do." She needed to make that clear, whether he believed it or not. "And yes, you're right, I conned you. But let me explain."

"Fine. Be my guest." He swept his hand across the report. "Explain away."

She started at the beginning, telling him how her

mother had come to Nashville to sell her songs. She also detailed how she'd gotten duped by his dad. "She wasn't a stalker. She was only trying to get him to make good on his promise. But he filed a restraining order against her instead, with you as his attorney." Mary paused, hoping for some empathy, but his expression remained hard and unyielding. "Mama fell apart after that. She was never the same. Her depression was so bad that she was barely parenting us anymore, and since Alice was so much younger than me, I tried to help raise her. But I was never able to influence my sister to stop hating Kirby for what he'd done to Mama. She was consumed with it. I got consumed, as well, with the pain he'd caused. I hated him, too."

Brandon lifted his eyebrows. "So you took your pain out on me?"

"At first we tried to cook up ways to get back at your dad, but none of them panned out. Then Alice devised a scheme for me to draw you in. She saw some posts on your social media pages that your friends were encouraging you to find a nice girl, so she suggested that I should present myself to you in that way. She kept saying that I was a good girl, anyway. That it wouldn't be much of a stretch for me."

"Christ," he muttered, tension in his voice. He wasn't softening at all.

"I was mixed up from the beginning and unsure of how far to take it. Mostly I just wanted to find out how responsible you were in what happened to Mama. And once I got close to you, I realized that you never would've hurt her purposely. But by then, I was already in too deep. I was already developing feelings for you."

"You never thought to contact me outright and discuss the stalking situation with your mom? To explain your side of it?"

"No. We never thought of that. But we didn't know if we could trust you. Alice is still convinced that you and your dad should pay for what he did to our mother. I know my sister is really messed up and I obviously was, too, for having done something like this. But I've been learning my lessons, and this is turning out to be the hardest one of all." Facing the fact she'd hurt someone she loved, she thought. That she'd damaged him.

He sat quietly for a moment, as if he was contemplating the whole ball of wax. Then he said, "If what you say is true and my father cheated your mother in a business deal and falsified the stalking charges, I'll make sure that he fixes it." He blew out a heavy sigh. "But I need to talk to him and get his side of the story. I can't just take you and Alice at your word. I mean, really, Mary, how am I supposed to trust anything you say?"

"You're not, I guess." She glanced down at her hands, twisting them on her lap. "But if I could take back what I did to you, I would." She lifted her gaze to meet his. "I was never comfortable with it. That's why I was always talking about breaking it off. At first I thought it would hurt you less for me to disappear and for you to never know the truth. But when we were in Texas and everything was going so beautifully with your family, I decided I was going to tell you the truth once we got back. I even thought that maybe we'd be able to stay together."

He looked at her as if she'd gone mad. "For all I know, this sorrowful act of yours is part of a new ploy to rein me in, to use me for my money or whatever it is you really want."

"It isn't." All she could do now was continue to tell him the truth and pray for him to understand. "Alice tried to convince me that I should marry you for your money. But I'm not interested in that. If I married you, it would be for love."

He scoffed at her response. "Sweet little Mary, ever the enchantress. Well, you know what? I was so bewitched by you I actually wondered what it would be like to make you my wife." He shook his head. "But it worried me, how I was falling in love with a stranger, a woman who wouldn't talk about her past."

"I'll tell you anything now, anything you want to know." Her heart hurt so badly, she feared it was going to shatter into a zillion pieces. Knowing that he'd considered marriage made it so much worse.

"I'm not interested in anything else you have to say." He stood and came around his desk, towering over her while she remained seated. "I'll talk to my dad and get back to you. But it'll be his version of the facts that I'll be relying on, not yours."

"I understand. But as far as I'm concerned, there's nothing you or your dad need to make up for. What I did to you was just as hurtful as what he did to my mom. And I'm so sorry, Brandon. So incredibly sorry."

"Stop with the apologies. It's not helping." He leaned against the edge of his desk. "It's too late for me to keep feeling something for you. It's too late for everything."

She wanted to curl up and cry, but she couldn't do that in front of him.

"You can go now," he said. "I trust you can see yourself out."

"Yes." She stood, remembering every warm and romantic moment she'd spent with him. But it was over now. There was nothing left, except the ache that came with losing the man she loved.

Mary cried for hours, until there were no tears left. Still, Alice kept watching her as if she might burst out bawling again.

They sat on their tiny patio with dusk blanketing the sky. Their apartment faced the street, and she could see cars going by.

Mary's breath hitched. Her face was swollen, and her eyes stung. But the real pain was in her heart. "If I would've told him sooner, if I would've come clean from the start, he wouldn't hate me the way he does."

Alice frowned. "He has no right to hate you, not after the way his father trashed Mama."

"He said that he's going to talk to Kirby and get his side of it. And if his dad confirms that it's true, he'll make sure that Kirby fixes it."

"*If* his dad confirms it? You know damned well

that he's going to lie and say that Mama was a stalker."

Mary thought about how sincere Kirby seemed at the wedding and how he kept saying he was trying to turn over a new leaf. "Maybe he'll tell the truth. Maybe he'll admit to what he did."

Alice shook her head. "That would take a miracle, and this isn't feeling like a miracle-type situation to me. And on top of that, Brandon should have forgiven you. Isn't that the way love is supposed to work?"

"I don't know enough about love to answer that question. But I was hoping and praying that he would forgive me." She'd already forgiven his father. After what she'd done to Brandon, she was in no position to judge Kirby.

Alice dragged a hand through her platinum hair. "So if by some unexpected chance Kirby does corroborate our story, what do you think Brandon meant by fixing it?"

"I have no idea."

"Do you think it would involve money?"

"I don't know." Money was the least of her concerns.

Her sister turned quiet. A fly buzzed by and she waved it away. Then she asked, "Do you still love him?"

"Yes." She couldn't deny the truth. "But I wish that I didn't, with how it's tearing me apart. You warned me that I was going to get hurt, and you were right."

"I didn't trust him any more than I trusted his dad, and now you're paying the ultimate price. It's not fair that you're suffering."

"Are you sure you care about how I feel?" Mary shooed away the same fly when it came near her. "Because with how mean you've been to me, I'm surprised you're not gloating over my pain."

Alice winced. "I'm sorry I acted like such a bitch. And I'm sorry that Brandon broke your heart." She leaned into the table. "Truly, I am. You've been a really good sister to me." Her voice quavered. "When I was a kid, I just wanted Mama to be well, to be there when I needed her. But you were the one who took care of me. I love you more than you know."

"Thank you." Even as messed up as Alice was, Mary could tell that her sister meant it. "I love you, too. But I wish we hadn't grown up hating Kirby." That hadn't done either of them any good. "Our lives shouldn't have been about that."

"I still think he owes us for what he did to Mama. If they offer us a financial settlement, I'm going to take every last dollar they're willing to part with."

"Money isn't my objective." For Mary, there were deeper issues at stake. "I'd like to see Mama's name cleared. And I'd like for Kirby to say he's sorry. That would be enough for me."

Her sister sighed. "I shouldn't have gotten you into this mess. I shouldn't have dragged you into something that wasn't right for you."

"I appreciate you saying that, but I made my own decisions."

Alice angled her head. "You don't think it's my fault? You're not blaming me?"

"No." Mary was responsible for what she'd done. "I kept lying to Brandon, even when I had feelings for him, even when I knew the destruction it could cause."

She'd alienated him all by herself.

Twelve

Brandon paced his dad's home studio, the place where the magic happened, where Kirby had recorded a good number of his albums. But this wasn't a magical day. He'd just confronted his dad about Cathy Birch and received a stunned look in return.

"She was Mary's mother?"

"Yes, I'm afraid she was." He stopped pacing and stood near a mixing board. "Was she a stalker? Was she harassing you?" Brandon remembered filing the restraining order. But he'd filed quite a few of them over the years. Cathy wasn't Kirby's only stalker—if she was one at all. "Tell me, Dad. Tell me exactly what transpired between you and Cathy."

Kirby grimaced. "It happened the way Mary said it did. The story she told you is accurate."

"Oh, God." If Brandon hadn't been standing so rigidly, his knees might've buckled. "What did you do? What did you make me do?"

"I'm sorry if I dragged you into a lie. But I was at my lowest then. Nothing in my life was going right. The drink and drugs were eating me alive."

"So you preyed on an innocent woman and offered to buy her songs? For what? The sex? The feeling of power?"

"It was all of that, I guess." Kirby rubbed a hand across his beard, his mouth set in a grim line. His eyes were partially shielded by the brim of his hat, his shirt collar turned up. "I took advantage of a lot of women in those days, and Cathy was no exception." He paused, his breathing rattled. "I wasn't lying to her about her songs, not at first. They were good, and they captured my attention. I wasn't going to record them myself. I was going to find a female artist who was better suited to them."

"But you were going to produce the project?"

"Yes. Except after I lost interest in Cathy, I lost interest in her music, too."

Heavens, above. Could his father have been any more of a jackass? "So you made her out to be a stalker?"

"She kept calling me, trying to get me to sign a contract with her, and I just wanted to be rid of her. I'd already moved on to someone else by then, so I convinced myself that she was harassing me."

Brandon could barely stand to be in the same room with his dad right now. None of this was tolerable. "When you were collecting stories for *Kirbyville*, you didn't stop to think to include her? To contact her and apologize? She was alive when you first started working on the book. You could've reached out to her then."

"Honestly? I forgot about her until now."

Everything inside Brandon was twisting and turning, tying his guts into knots. "You forgot? That's a lame-ass excuse."

"I know. But there was so much material for the book, and I was focused on family when I wrote it. I'm so sorry that her daughters suffered because of it. And I'm sorry that Mary hurt you."

"I don't want to talk about what Mary did to me." Brandon couldn't bear the ache it caused. He couldn't get past the knowledge that he'd fallen for a woman who'd used him for revenge. All these years, all this time, he'd never been in love. Then along came Mary with her warm and gentle ways, with her mystery, with her deception.

"Tell me what you want me to do, and I'll do it," his dad said, cutting into his thoughts.

"I want you to offer to buy Cathy's songs from Mary and Alice and find a female artist to record them, like you first promised to do. It's imperative that you help make their mother's music a success. I also want you to make a public announcement and admit what you did to Cathy. Of course, I expect you to apologize to her daughters privately. You can't skip that."

"Do you think they'll forgive me?"

"I don't know." Brandon couldn't predict anyone's behavior anymore.

"Are you going to forgive Mary for lying to you about who she was?"

"That's none of your concern."

"Yes, it is. You're my son, and I want to see you happy. If you love her, you should forgive her."

Brandon shook his head. His father was the last person he wanted advice from. "Don't stick your nose into my affairs, not after the havoc you caused."

"But you're a peacemaker, and you need to make peace with this."

"I am making peace with it." He stood and moved about the studio again, feeling trapped by the familiarity of his surroundings. When he was a kid he used to marvel at being here, listening to his dad record. Even back then, Brandon had wanted to be part of it somehow. But not like this, never like this. "I'm going to draw up the paperwork with the terms of your offer and arrange a meeting with Mary and Alice at my office. I'll need for you to be there, too."

"Of course." Kirby sounded more than agreeable. "Whatever you require."

Brandon sighed. "I'll advise them to bring their own attorney. I'm sure they'll find someone reputable to represent them." He didn't doubt that Alice would seek out the best.

"That's good, but that's not what I meant about you making peace with Mary."

"It's the best I can do." It was all he could do, he thought, short of telling Mary that he still loved her.

And he hurt too badly to do that. Brandon was keeping his bruised and battered heart to himself.

Mary and Alice arrived at Brandon's office with Christine Norseman, a hard-hitting lawyer Alice had procured. Only Mary wasn't thinking about the business deal that was coming their way. She was blinded by the sight of the man she loved.

Brandon looked tall and dark and professional in a gray suit and burgundy tie. When he reached out to shake everyone's hand, Mary felt weak. By the time his hand enveloped hers, she could barely breathe. For a moment, she felt the electrical charge running between them.

Their gazes met, but neither of them spoke. She couldn't think of a single thing to say that didn't involve missing him. He broke the handshake and glanced away, leaving her staring after him.

He offered them a seat and said, "My dad is on his way. He's running a few minutes late." He then asked, "Can I get anyone anything?" He motioned to the bar in his office. "Coffee, juice, water, soda?"

Christine went for an apple juice and Alice took a soda. Mary didn't want anything, except for Brandon to love her once again.

Soon Kirby dashed in, carrying two single red roses. He handed one to Mary and offered the other to Alice. Her sister refused to take it. Mary gathered it up with hers, placing both flowers on her lap.

He sat down and said to them, "I'm so sorry for the pain I caused your family. Your mother deserved better and so did you girls. I hope that someday you'll find it in your hearts to forgive me."

"I already do," Mary replied, and exchanged a gentle glance with him.

He thanked her with an appreciative nod of his head, and the room went quiet. Until Alice said to him, "Mary doesn't want me to keep hating you. But I still do." She turned toward Mary. "I'm not like you. I can't forgive that easily. I just can't."

Kirby nodded and said to Alice, "It's all right. I accept however you feel. But before we get to the business part of this meeting, I want to tell you what I remember about your mother." He addressed both sisters. "She was kind and trusting and far too good for someone like me. We didn't talk about our children. We kept our kids out of it. But I'll bet if we'd shared that information, she would've told me how spunky her youngest was." He chanced a smile at Alice. "I admire your grit." He gestured to her cow-punk garb. "I like your retro vibe, too."

"Oh, right." She scowled at him. "The snake oil salesman, trying to win me over. Our mother didn't stand a chance with you."

"No, she didn't. But you do. If I had a daughter, I'd want her to be like you, Alice." He said to Mary, "I'd be pleased to have you as part of my family, too."

Her eyes nearly flooded with tears. She could tell that he was giving her his blessing to be with Brandon, if his son were inclined to be with her.

She glanced over at her former lover, but he just

cleared his throat and said, "I think we should discuss the offer now."

"Yes, let's do that," Christine replied. She was a fiftysomething blonde with a no-nonsense personality, ready to get this show on the road.

So was Alice, it seemed. She perked up, obviously anxious for the negotiations to begin. But even so, she kept shooting Kirby sideways glances. It made Mary wonder if she was secretly impressed with the way he'd praised her. With Alice, it was difficult to tell. But even so, Mary didn't see her sister forgiving him anytime soon.

The offer involved an astronomical amount of money to purchase Mama's songs and market them. Christine went over the fine print and suggested a few changes. Brandon and Kirby agreed. They seemed willing to do whatever they could to give Alice and Mary what Kirby should have given Mama all those years ago.

But Mary didn't want the money. She'd already made up her mind about that. "I'd like to sign my share over to Alice," she said. "But with the stipulation that she gives my portion to charity." She gazed at her sister. "I want you to choose a charity that will be meaningful to you." She thought it was important for Alice to learn to do some good in the world. "Are you willing to do that?"

"Of course," Alice replied. "But are you sure you don't want to keep some of it for yourself?"

"I'm positive." Mary wasn't interested in a payout, and she never would be. She shifted in her chair and asked Christine, "Can we add a clause to the contract about the charity?"

"Definitely." The attorney made a note of it.

Mary spoke to Kirby. "I'm glad that you're going to make a public announcement to clear Mama's name. We worked really hard to hide the harassment charges from everyone she knew. But it was still a stain on her psyche. It's important that you're going to let the world know that she didn't do anything wrong."

"The public announcement was Brandon's idea," Kirby said. "I can't take credit for that. But I'm more than willing to admit my wrongdoings to the press."

"Good," Christine said, chiming in to the conversation. "Now we can proceed and get all of this enforced."

Yes, Mary thought. They needed to proceed. She looked across the desk at Brandon. He was watching her with a tortured expression, a frown that appeared to be emerging straight from his soul.

An ache Mary could feel, too.

He called in his assistant to make the necessary changes, and the contract was revised. Once it was ready, the lawyers went over it again, making sure everything was correct.

And that was it. The parties involved signed it.

As the group prepared to part ways, Kirby reached out to hug Mary. She buried her face against his shoulder and wished it was Brandon wrapping her in his embrace.

But he merely stood back in silence. Kirby released her, and she turned and spoke to Brandon.

"Take care of yourself," she said.

"You, too," he replied, his voice low and unbearably soft.

Steeped in her loss, Mary headed for the door. But she couldn't stop herself from glancing back at Brandon.

Just to fill her vision with him one last time.

Brandon spent as much time as he could with Zoe. Being with the baby gave him comfort. But being around her made him long for what he'd lost, too.

The possibility of a future, of a family. He couldn't imagine ever feeling about anyone the way he'd felt about Mary, but that was over now. Two weeks had passed since he'd seen her at the meeting and he still couldn't face the truth of what she'd done to him. He remained hurt and angry and confused, with a hole clawing its way through his heart.

Today he was at Tommy's place, in Zoe's pink and puffy nursery, rocking her while she made cute little baby sounds. His brother stood nearby, watching him.

Tommy said, "With the way you've been monopolizing my kid, I think you need to hurry up and have one of your own."

"Yeah, as if it's just that easy." Brandon gazed at his niece and the flowery headband she wore. Tommy had dressed her up for Brandon's visit.

"I'm sorry that it didn't work out between you and

Mary. I know how tough it's been for you. But I'll bet she's really broken up over it, too."

Brandon didn't want to think about how badly she was hurting, not with how much he ached. "I've always been so careful, protecting myself and our family. I asked her when we first met if she knew who I was, but she lied to me, every damned step of the way."

"I know. But a lot has happened since then."

A lot of pain, Brandon thought, a lot of heartache, with what felt like no end in sight. "Dad is going to make the public announcement about Mary's mom next week. He's got a press conference lined up."

"That's good. By the way, I heard that Alice rented a luxurious new condo."

Brandon cocked his head. "Who told you that?"

"Dad found out from Mary. He's been keeping in touch with her. Alice is still leery of him, but he and Mary are becoming genuine friends. Dad didn't tell you because he's trying to keep you out of his relationship with Mary."

Brandon wasn't surprised that they'd gotten close. He'd seen their bond at their meeting. He'd watched his dad hug her and felt the sting of not being able to hold her himself. "So Mary is alone at their old apartment?"

"Yes, but she wants to be by herself. She wasn't interested in moving into the condo with Alice."

Brandon had been spending a lot of time alone, too, except for when he was here with Tommy and the baby. He got up and placed Zoe in her crib. She was drifting off to sleep. To keep her comfortable, he removed her headband.

He and Tommy walked onto the balcony, letting the baby settle into her dreams. It was nice outside, with a warm breeze.

"Maybe I should go see Mary," Brandon said. "Not to rekindle our romance, but to at least find a way to forgive her." He didn't want to keep wallowing in this. It was just too damned painful. "I think it's what we're both going to need to move on."

"Then do it, bro. Do whatever you have to do to get through this. I don't want to see you hurting. Or Mary, either. It's not a good way to live. I agree that you both need closure."

"Thanks." He sucked in his breath. "I'm going to head out now." Before he took the coward's way out and lost his nerve. Because deep down, he was still afraid of the effect she had on him.

He left Tommy's house and drove straight to her apartment. Once he got there and knocked on the door, he discovered that she wasn't home. But then he realized that she was probably still at work, and he'd showed up a little too early to see her. He sat on the stoop and waited, with a lump in his throat.

A short time later, her car pulled up. She got out, her footsteps stalling as she neared the front door. Clearly, she was shocked to see him. For a moment, she just stared.

Then she said, "Brandon?"

"Hey." He stood and dusted himself off. He felt like a bubble-brained boy, lacking the finesse he needed to pull this off. Even as a youth, he'd never been this awkward. "I was hoping we could talk."

She hesitated before she asked, "Do you want to come in?"

"Sure." He tried to seem more casual than he felt.

She unlocked the door, and he followed her inside. She was wearing her bakery uniform, a plain white smock and loose pants. Her hair was neatly braided. He thought about the countless times he'd played with her hair. He wanted to move closer, to put his hands on her, to inhale her sugary scent.

"Sweet tea?"

He jerked to attention. "I'm sorry. What?"

"Would you like some sweet tea?"

"No, thanks." He went ahead and moved closer. They were standing in her living room, with the blinds drawn. "I'm just here to make things right. To forgive you, Mary, and stop both of us from hurting. I can't go on, aching the way I am, and neither can you."

Her gaze searched his. "So this isn't about us getting back together?"

"No." He reached out to skim his fingertips along her cheek. "It's just about finding some peace in all of this."

Her breath hitched. "Is touching me making you feel peaceful, Brandon?"

He shook his head. His ache was actually getting stronger. "You have the softest skin, the most innocent face. It's still hard for me to believe that you tricked me."

"I'm so sorry I deceived you."

"I know you are." He didn't doubt her sincerity. The truth was in her eyes. "I owe you an apology, too. I shouldn't have brought you to my office that day under false pretenses. I shouldn't have blind-sided you that way."

"I understand how hurt and angry you were."

"I'm not angry anymore." He still ached inside, but that might never go away. "I should leave now." He removed his hand from her cheek. "I did what I came to do." To forgive her, he thought. Unfortunately, it hadn't brought him the closure it should have. She didn't look as if she felt much better, either. He backed away from her.

Now what was he supposed to say? Tell her to have a good life without him? He didn't know what parting words to use.

"Maybe you can stay a little longer," she said, her voice coming out choppy.

"What for?" he asked. He sounded disjointed, too. This reunion definitely wasn't going well.

She shrugged, a little too heavily, like a butterfly trying to lift its damaged wings. "I made chocolate chip cookies last night. You can have some with me."

"Cookies won't solve this."

"What will?"

"I don't know." But suddenly he didn't want to go. He didn't want to walk away and leave her be-hind. But he couldn't seem to find the strength to stay, either.

Before he could head for the door, she said, "Alice moved out. I live here alone now."

He cleared his throat and replied, "Tommy told me that she rented a condo. He said you've been talking to my dad a lot, too."

She nodded. "We've become really close."

It was strange how his father managed to make peace with her, but Brandon couldn't seem to do it. He was still so lost, so confused.

She bit down on her bottom lip. "He let me cry to him every night on the phone."

His heart tightened in his chest. Clearly, she'd been crying because of him. "I'll bet you never envisioned becoming friends with my dad."

"It's nice that he's been there for me. But it's still been hard, dealing with all of this." She glanced down at the floor. "I never should have done what I did to you."

"You don't have to keep apologizing." He couldn't bear to see more of her sorrow. She looked as lost as he felt.

She lifted her gaze, fractured as it was. "I told Kirby that I would try to help him find someone to date. I think he's ready for a new relationship. I believe that he's a changed man."

Brandon wanted to be a changed man, too, to be free of the pain. But he didn't know how to do it. "I should go." He couldn't stay. He was only making both of them suffer.

"I can walk you out."

"No. That's okay." He needed to make a clean

break. "Thanks for letting me come in and say what I needed to say." Even if it hadn't helped, he thought.

She stepped back. "I'll see you." She spoke softly, sadly.

"I'll see you, too." He didn't know when or if he would ever see her again, but it seemed like the proper thing to say.

He left her condo and climbed into his car. He was parked in a nearby guest spot, with a view of her front door. He suspected she might be on the verge of crying now, with tears flooding her eyes. Had he made it worse by coming here?

So what was he waiting for? He should get on the road, escaping as fast as his luxury sedan would take him. But he just sat behind the wheel, mired in pain and torment.

He glanced at Mary's door. He couldn't deny that he loved her. That he needed her. That he wanted her.

So what was he going to do about it?

Be the guy who fixes it, he told himself, *with the woman he loves by his side.*

Brandon got out of his car and returned to her apartment. He rang the bell, his pulse pounding in his ears.

She answered the summons, and he sucked in his breath. She did look as if she'd been crying.

"Do you still love me, Mary?" he asked. He was certain that she did, but he needed to hear it.

"Yes." She shivered where she stood. "God, yes."

"I still love you, too." He couldn't stop the rush of

emotion that poured through him, admitting how he felt, letting her know what was going on inside him.

"Are you sure?" she asked. "Because I couldn't take it if you…"

"I'm positive." He knew what was in his heart, and he knew that living without her wasn't an option. He reached out to her. "Let's start over. As friends, as lovers, as everything we should've been before, but without any lies or secrets between us."

"I can't imagine anything better." She stepped forward, into the circle of his arms. "I've missed you so badly."

"Me, too." He'd barely been surviving without her.

She cried a little, but he knew they were happy tears, not the sad ones from before.

They both went silent, steeped in the commitment they'd just made. He closed his eyes and rocked her in his arms, her sweet scent enveloping him.

She lifted her head and whispered, "Make love with me, Brandon. Be with me."

He accepted her invitation, and she led him to her room. He was never going to lose her again.

They undressed each other, slowly, wanting to make the moment last. They kissed and got into bed. He glanced up and saw the fairy painting he'd given her, intensifying the magic.

He caressed her, filling his hands with her body. She touched him, too, in the most intimate of ways.

She had protection readily available. "I bought it a while ago," she said. "In case you ever spent the night here."

He took the packet, but he didn't open it right away. For now, he wanted to profess more of his feelings, more of what the future would entail. "I want you to move in with me." He breathed her in, all the way to his soul. "I want to sleep beside you each night and wake up next to you every morning."

"I'll be there, whenever you need me." She pressed closer to him. "I want all of those same things."

He finally put on the condom and entered her, letting the sensation of being inside her engulf him. She moaned when he pushed deeper, and they made love. In the middle of the day.

Together at last.

As they lay naked, sated from the sex, Mary smiled at her man. *Her man.* Oh, how she loved the sound of that.

Finally, they got up and slipped on their clothes. She didn't put her uniform back on. She chose a simple white sundress from her closet.

"I can't wait to see you in a gown," he said.

"At a charity ball?" She was prepared to learn to waltz and meet his friends, to be part of everything that was Brandon.

"Actually, I was talking about our wedding." He sat on the edge of the bed and swept her onto his lap.

Her heartbeat skittered. "We're getting married?"

"We are if you'll have me. I want to do more than just live together. I want to take vows, too. But we can take our time and do it right. We don't have to rush." He looked into her eyes. "Will you become my wife? Will you do me the honor?"

"I absolutely will." She kissed him slowly, romantically. She could kiss him for a thousand years and never get enough. Afterward, she said, "I think taking our time is a good idea. We need to relax and get to know each other better. I was hiding who I was before, and now I'm going to be the real me."

He nodded. "I'm looking forward to knowing the real you." He nuzzled her cheek. "I'm already getting attached to her."

Mary sighed. This was the best day of her life. Their relationship had started off wrong, but it was perfect now. He was perfect, too, her future husband. No matter what obstacles they faced, they would always have each other.

"After we have kids, we can move into my country house," he said. He hesitated. "You want kids, don't you?"

She quickly replied, "Yes, of course." She wanted to create a family, especially with him. "But when I was growing up, I never really understood motherhood."

"Because of how depressed your mom was?"

"I know she was hurting. But I wish she would have sought help instead of shutting everyone out. I still worry about Alice, too, and how wild she is."

Brandon gazed at her with admiration, with depth and care. "You're a good sister. She's lucky she has you. But getting our families together is going to be tough, with how much Alice probably still hates my dad." He frowned a little. "Do you think she's ever going to accept him?"

"I don't know, but he's going to try to develop a working relationship with her. He wants to get her input on what artist should record Mama's songs."

"I think that's a great idea."

"So do I." She hoped that it would help give her sister some direction. She knew how important those songs were to Alice. They still meant the world to Mary, too.

"Dad is going to be thrilled when we tell him that we're engaged."

"I'd love for him to walk me down the aisle, the way he did for Sophie. I'd also like for Alice to be my maid of honor and help me choose a dress. So one way or another, she's going to have to get used to the Talbots."

"Considering that you'll be one of us?" He smiled, lifted her hand. "You and I need to shop for a diamond."

"It doesn't have to be anything overly fancy, but do you think I could have a sapphire or something blue? I want a ring the color of your eyes."

"That makes me feel good. But maybe it could be just a little bit fancy. I'm excited about giving you sparkly things. Come to think of it, there are blue diamonds. So maybe we could look into that, along with sapphires or any other stone you want. We can design it together."

"Thank you. That sounds fun. We can choose whatever feels right and put it all together."

"Marrying you feels right. Being the father to your children feels right." He paused and asked, "Do you think I should use Cline as my best man?"

She sputtered into a jovial laugh. "That would be adorable."

He laughed, too. Then he said, "Sharing my life with you is all that matters. I can't wait for you to move in with me."

"I'll pack today." She wanted nothing more than to be Brandon's partner. Her heart was glowing, from the inside out.

"Things are going to be interesting, with us figuring it out as we go."

She thought about the world in which he'd been raised. "Maybe I can become a pastry chef for the rich and famous. Maybe that can be my new career. I'm going to get a lot of experience dealing with that crowd."

"You can do anything you want, Mary. You're as talented as anyone I know."

In the sweet silence that followed, he slanted his mouth over hers, and they kissed once again. She settled in his arms. No matter what the future held, they were both willing to do their best to make it work.

Sealing their fate forever.

* * * * *

*Don't miss a single book
in the Sons of Country series
by Sheri WhiteFeather!*

Wrangling the Rich Rancher
Nashville Rebel
Nashville Secrets

Available from Harlequin Desire.

COMING NEXT MONTH FROM

HARLEQUIN®
Desire

Available April 2, 2019

#2653 NEED ME, COWBOY

Copper Ridge • by Maisey Yates

Unfairly labeled by his family's dark reputation, brooding rancher Levi Tucker is done playing by the rules. He demands a new mansion designed by famous architect Faith Grayson, an innocent beauty he would only corrupt...but he *must* have her.

#2654 WILD RIDE RANCHER

Texas Cattleman's Club: Houston • by Maureen Child

Rancher Liam Morrow doesn't trust rich beauty Chloe Hemsworth *or* want to deal with her new business. But when they're trapped by a flash flood, heated debates turn into a wild affair. For the next two weeks, can she prove him wrong without falling for him?

#2655 TEMPORARY TO TEMPTED

The Bachelor Pact • by Jessica Lemmon

Andrea *really* regrets bribing a hot stranger to be her fake wedding date... especially because he's her new boss! But Gage offers a deal: he'll do it in exchange for her not quitting. As long as love isn't involved, he's game...except he can't resist her!

#2656 HIS FOR ONE NIGHT

First Family of Rodeo • by Sarah M. Anderson

When a surprise reunion leads to a one-night stand with Nashville sweetheart Brooke, Flash wants to turn one night into more... But when the rodeo star learns she's been hiding his child, can he trust her, especially when he's made big mistakes of his own?

#2657 ENGAGING THE ENEMY

The Bourbon Brothers • by Reese Ryan

Sexy Parker Abbott wants *more* of her family's land? Kayleigh Jemison refuses—unless he pays double *and* plays her fake boyfriend to trick her ex. Money is no problem, but can he afford desiring the beautiful woman who hates everything his family represents?

#2658 VENGEFUL VOWS

Marriage at First Sight • by Yvonne Lindsay

Peyton wants revenge on Galen's family. And she'll get it through an arranged marriage between them. But Galen is not what she expected, and soon she's sharing his bed and his life...until secrets come to light that will change everything!

YOU CAN FIND MORE INFORMATION ON UPCOMING HARLEQUIN® TITLES,
FREE EXCERPTS AND MORE AT WWW.HARLEQUIN.COM.

HDCNM0319

Get 4 FREE REWARDS!

We'll send you 2 FREE Books plus 2 FREE Mystery Gifts.

Harlequin® Desire books feature heroes who have it all: wealth, status, incredible good looks... everything but the right woman.

FREE
Value Over
$20

YES! Please send me 2 FREE Harlequin® Desire novels and my 2 FREE gifts (gifts are worth about $10 retail). After receiving them, if I don't wish to receive any more books, I can return the shipping statement marked "cancel." If I don't cancel, I will receive 6 brand-new novels every month and be billed just $4.55 per book in the U.S. or $5.24 per book in Canada. That's a savings of at least 13% off the cover price! It's quite a bargain! Shipping and handling is just 50¢ per book in the U.S. and 75¢ per book in Canada.* I understand that accepting the 2 free books and gifts places me under no obligation to buy anything. I can always return a shipment and cancel at any time. The free books and gifts are mine to keep no matter what I decide.

225/326 HDN GMYU

Name (please print)

Address   Apt. #

City   State/Province   Zip/Postal Code

Mail to the **Reader Service:**
IN U.S.A.: P.O. Box 1341, Buffalo, NY 14240-8531
IN CANADA: P.O. Box 603, Fort Erie, Ontario L2A 5X3

Want to try 2 free books from another series! Call 1-800-873-8635 or visit www.ReaderService.com.

Unfairly labeled by his family's dark reputation, brooding rancher Levi Tucker is done playing by the rules. He demands a new mansion designed by famous architect Faith Grayson, an innocent beauty he would only corrupt...but he must *have her.*

Read on for a sneak peek at
Need Me, Cowboy
by New York Times *bestselling author Maisey Yates!*

Faith had designed buildings that had changed skylines, and she'd done homes for the rich and the famous.

Levi Tucker was something else. He was infamous.

The self-made millionaire who had spent the past five years in prison and was now digging his way back...

He wanted her. And yeah, it interested her.

She let out a long, slow breath as she rounded the final curve on the mountain driveway, the vacant lot coming into view. But it wasn't the lot, or the scenery surrounding it, that stood out in her vision first and foremost. No, it was the man, with his hands shoved into the pockets of his battered jeans, worn cowboy boots on his feet. He had on a black T-shirt, in spite of the morning chill, and a black cowboy hat was pressed firmly on his head.

She had researched him, obviously. She knew what he looked like, but she supposed she hadn't had a sense of…the scale of him.

Strange, because she was usually pretty good at picking up on those kinds of things in photographs.

And yet, she had not been able to accurately form a picture of the man in her mind. And when she got out of the car, she was struck by the way he seemed to fill this vast, empty space.

That also didn't make any sense.

He was big. Over six feet and with broad shoulders, but he didn't fill this space. Not literally.

But she could feel his presence as soon as the cold air wrapped itself around her body upon exiting the car.

And when his ice-blue eyes connected with hers, she drew in a breath. She was certain he filled her lungs, too.

Because that air no longer felt cold. It felt hot. Impossibly so.

Because those blue eyes burned with something.

Rage. Anger.

Not at her—in fact, his expression seemed almost friendly.

But there was something simmering beneath the surface…and it had touched her already.

Don't miss what happens next!
Need Me, Cowboy
by New York Times *bestselling author Maisey Yates.*

Available April 2019 wherever
Harlequin® Desire books and ebooks are sold.

www.Harlequin.com

Want to give in to temptation with
steamy tales of irresistible desire?

Check out **Harlequin® Presents®**,
Harlequin® Desire and
Harlequin® Kimani™ Romance books!

New books available every month!

CONNECT WITH US AT:

Facebook.com/groups/HarlequinConnection

Facebook.com/HarlequinBooks

Twitter.com/HarlequinBooks

Instagram.com/HarlequinBooks

Pinterest.com/HarlequinBooks

ReaderService.com

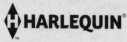

**ROMANCE WHEN
YOU NEED IT**

PGENRE2018

Love Harlequin romance?

DISCOVER.

Be the first to find out about promotions, news and exclusive content!

f Facebook.com/HarlequinBooks

▼ Twitter.com/HarlequinBooks

◉ Instagram.com/HarlequinBooks

Ⓟ Pinterest.com/HarlequinBooks

ReaderService.com

EXPLORE.

Sign up for the Harlequin e-newsletter and download a free book from any series at **TryHarlequin.com.**

CONNECT.

Join our Harlequin community to share your thoughts and connect with other romance readers!
Facebook.com/groups/HarlequinConnection

⬢ HARLEQUIN®

**ROMANCE WHEN
YOU NEED IT**

HSOCIAL2018

THE WORLD IS BETTER WITH
Romance

Harlequin has everything from contemporary, passionate and heartwarming to suspenseful and inspirational stories.

Whatever your mood, we have a romance just for you!

Connect with us to find your next great read, special offers and more.

f /HarlequinBooks

🐦 @HarlequinBooks

www.HarlequinBlog.com

www.Harlequin.com/Newsletters

❖ HARLEQUIN®

A *Romance* FOR EVERY MOOD™

www.Harlequin.com